FREER'S COVE

by
Ethel Gordon

COWARD, McCANN & GEOGHEGAN, INC.
NEW YORK

FREER'S COVE

I

1

UP TO THAT MORNING when I first set eyes on Amos Freer I had never even heard of Freer's Cove, in the state of Maine. Nothing could have seemed more unlikely than that I was about to become part of that remote place, that the lives of the Freers would soon be inextricably bound up with my own.

But wait.

Maybe it more properly began the morning before, when Dr. Service told me I was pregnant. Or maybe even before that, maybe it began during those months when Jed and I were growing increasingly aware that our marriage was a failure and, what was even more painful, that neither of us was interested in saving it.

Marrying had been a mindless, spontaneous act, a result of a summer of blissful weekends at Jones Beach, sun and ocean and desirable suntanned flesh, and the wonder of two lonely people finding each other. Jed was a Mississippian, studying law in New York. I was in my junior year. I had come to New York after my mother had died suddenly of a heart attack in Springfield, Illinois, our home. She left me only enough money to take me to New York and pay for those first two years at the university.

I suppose we were each hungering for love, for belonging to someone. I suppose we believed that marriage would be a prolonged weekend at Jones Beach. How practical it would be! we thought, when we gave any thought to the practical: We could pool our money from our part-time jobs and student loans. We married in too great a haste to find out if our personalities were compatible, our likes and dislikes harmonious. How could we even imagine that the more we knew each other, the less we would admire each other?

The baby was not planned as a ploy to save our marriage. The baby was a stupid accident: We continued to share our bed, sometimes drawing close in a purely physical impulse even when emotionally we were far apart.

So, on that climactic morning when I stared at Dr. Service, I heard myself say in consternation, "But it can't be!"

"There's always abortion," said Dr. Service, looking bored. "This would be the easiest time to perform it. I assume you are not married."

"I *am* married."

The doctor put down my card. "Let me know what you decide to do."

I left his office. I walked endlessly that day through the narrow streets of the Village, unable to bring myself to go to class. Exhausted, I sat down in Washington Square Park and watched the children playing and tried to imagine that one of them was mine. Impossible. I found myself talking aloud and checked myself, looking around to see if I'd been over-heard. I could still make educational psych if I got up now. But I couldn't. What was the point?

I tried to organize my thinking logically, which does not come easy to me. Even if the marriage had worked out, we could not afford a baby now. Both Jed and I had student loans that would take years to repay. Jed still had another year of law school after this one. In his spare time he clerked in a law office, earning enough for our rent and his clothes, an important aspect of his life. My job in the university library took care of our food and what passed for my ward-robe. I would be getting my degree in June and planned on taking my master's next year at night so I could work full time during the day. Now and then I would wonder if maybe if we'd had some extra money to soften our grinding poverty, we might not always be at each other's throats. But then I would think: If we really loved each other, how important would poverty be compared to having each other? And the next thought, inevitably, how much *do* we love each other? Do we love each other at all? Did we ever?

Get back to the problem at hand. My thoughts were too much given to straying, even before. Whom could we fall back on for help, if we decided to go ahead with the baby, for some inexplicable reason?

Jed's father, like Jed, had a taste for luxury and no income to provide it. His brother envied him his education; his sisters had made it plain that they thought he had no busi-ness taking a wife before he was able to support her. I had an aunt in Jacksonville who lived on a pension and some relatives on the West Coast who only knew me by name. I was an only child. We were both waifs in a strange city. If this had been the impelling force in our marrying, it now offered us no help in staying together.

It was after six when I finally let myself into our apartment. I had waited this long deliberately. Jed came home at four thirty, and we had dinner at five so he could be at work by six. He would be angry at my not being home to fix dinner; there would be exasperated words when he returned at eleven. But I could not face him with the news yet.

The apartment was breathless. We were agonizing through a September heat wave more oppressive than July. The windows were closed because they were level with the sidewalk, and anyone could have slipped in. Papers and books lay scattered on the two kitchen tables that served us as desks. There was a smell of frankfurters and beans, which meant that Jed had found a can to open for his dinner. The smell was nauseating. It was too hot to eat. I opened the windows and sat in the dark, watching the legs of people passing by. After a while I drew the shades and lit the lamp and made myself some iced tea.

As Dr. Service had said, there was always abortion.

It was now legal in New York State; it could be done without danger to the mother. We would have to raise the money for the hospital; maybe Jed could get an advance in salary from his boss. There was that money we had saved for a skiing week in December. Only—

Only I am crazy. Jed has told me that, fondly now and then when he enjoys my craziness, but angrily most of the time when he says I get him into difficult situations. It was crazy to fight the only practical solution to the problem. The truth was: I did not want to abort the baby.

I knew little about the fetus alive within me, not even if it were legally alive, but it was our flesh, Jed's and mine. We were responsible for it. I could not accept the idea of killing it. There it was. I am crazy, but there it was.

I made myself another glass of iced tea and sipped it, perspiring, staring into nothing. There was an alternative, if I were crazy enough to have the baby, *if* Jed would agree. There was adoption. There were kind agencies who screened would-be parents through the most searching of examinations, who would come up with a good, decent, loving, substantial couple to take our baby and bring it up as their own. A sensible mother, an unselfish warm father—it would probably fare better than it might with us. God knew it would be more secure: How long would Jed and I continue to live this farce of a marriage together? Maybe only until we saved enough to put one of us on a plane to Mexico for a quick divorce. Was it fair to a baby to start it off in life without a father? Better adoption.

Yes, adoption.

My second glass of tea was still unfinished when Jed let himself in. I stared at him blankly, as if his reality were too confounding after all the thinking I had done about him.

Jed is very attractive, and he knows it. When he caught my stare, his hand went automatically to his dark hair, smoothing it. He had spent sixty-five dollars for that jacket, which couldn't even be worn once the weather turned cold. I suppose what really hurt me was that Jed had told me I looked like a ragamuffin and for heaven's sake to buy myself a dress, but instead of splitting the sixty-five dollars, he blew it all on that jacket. Fortunately I am tall and so look thinner than I am, and whatever rag I wear hangs well, even what I pick up from the thrift shop down the street. In Springfield I worked one summer as a model in a downtown store.

Jed returned my stare. "Okay, something's up. What is it?"

It had to be said. It would take his mind off my not being home to make his dinner. I took a breath. "I went to the doctor today. He said I was pregnant."

"Damn," he said quietly, and sat down on the couch.

We stared at each other bleakly.

"Do you realize what an abortion costs? Where are we going to get the money?"

"We might have to do without a winter jacket," I said in a kind of wild despair.

"Did I ever tell you you're a jealous bitch?"

"Often."

"We agreed that you buy your clothes out of your own money. Leave my clothes out of the discussion."

He has this charming Mississippi speech. Sometimes I had to concentrate to realize what he was saying, his savageries could sound so charming.

I said, "I paid for the mattress with my money because you said you were short. You sleep on the mattress, too." You started a baby on that mattress, too.

"They raised the rent fifteen dollars, remember?"

It was so ugly. I felt so ugly. He sounded so ugly. We were so ugly together. The tragic thing was that maybe if we were each married to someone else, the ugliness wouldn't have had a reason to surface. I wanted to weep.

He said, "Take the money we saved for that ski trip. I'll try to borrow the rest from the guys in the office."

I don't know why I went to him and leaned against him.

Maybe because he was shouldering the responsibility for the baby, maybe some atavistic impulse rising from the pregnancy, or some association instilled by books and movies in which the announcement of a forthcoming baby is an occasion for tenderness, or perhaps just plain hopelessness at the plight we found ourselves in, but I put my arm through his and took his hand and said, "Jed, listen."

He allowed me to hold his hand, but suspiciously.

"Jed, I've been thinking for twelve hours. Suppose we were to have the baby—"

He drew back sharply. "You're crazy. Daisy, you are really crazy."

It rhymed. Crazy Daisy.

"Look, I didn't mean we should keep it after I had it. Only that maybe we shouldn't destroy it. But we'd give it up for adoption right away. I understand they even pay the expenses of having it, good reliable agencies do. I remember the Bladers from Springfield came to New York to adopt a baby, and they were telling us how the mother is taken care of until—"

"You are crazy."

"You won't even listen to what I'm saying! It wouldn't interfere with us for more than the last few months, and then—"

"I hear you. Loud and clear. Daisy, you agreed that when we got married, there wouldn't be any children, not for years, not until we both had a chance to live a little—"

"I didn't plan the baby any more than you did! But it's started—"

"So finish it!" he said savagely.

He wrenched his arm free and went over to the closet to

undress. He was furious, but not so furious that he didn't search for his specially shaped hanger for his jacket. I watched dumbly while he wrenched off his shirt and threw it on the closet floor for me to take to the laundromat on Saturday.

"Goddamn," he said, not even turning to look at me, "for years I've been working my ass off to get through this goddamn school, to get my hands on a few extra bucks so maybe I can start living a little. If you think you're going to kill it all so you can have a baby—"

"I told you. I don't *want* it. We'll give it up for adoption. I just don't want to . . . to destroy it."

"You know something, Daisy? I don't trust you, not one little bit. You're tricky. You'd trick me into keeping it the way you tricked me when you said you didn't want any babies. But I'm not having any more, hear? I've had enough of this crappy joint—"

Oh, I knew as well as he how sad and dingy that room was. I swept and dusted it once a week, didn't I? I'd tried to camouflage it with bright cushions on the mud-colored sofa and posters on the cracked walls, but it was still sad and dingy. Still, it was where we loved each other, or at least had loved each other once. His words made that love as sad and dingy as the room, but maybe it was only the truth.

"Will this doctor you went to do it for you in his office? It'll be cheaper that way than in a hospital—"

I longed to run away, anywhere, away from him, but where was there to run to at midnight on West Tenth Street in New York without any money? The only place even to hide from him was our small excuse for a bathroom: I rushed inside and wept.

Logic told me he was right. Anyone would be out of his mind to bring a baby into this world under these circumstances. Out of *her* mind. Crazy Daisy.

He knocked on the door. He was tired; he was disgusted; there was no pity in his voice when he said, "Get the hell out of there, Daisy. I want to shave."

He shaved at night, because he had an eight thirty class like me and it was hard to get out of bed in the morning. I washed my face hastily and brushed my teeth and opened the door and went past him and got into bed. He shaved, and brushed his teeth, and turned out the lights, and climbed into bed beside me. When we turned in our sleep, we touched, and I felt his breath on my bare shoulder, felt his arm flung out unconsciously across my hips. I slept and woke, and slept and woke, and each time I woke I thought: I must get out, this is a mockery, sharing this bed. Let him keep the room, I must leave, I'll get a full-time job and support myself as long as I can and then let the agency take over. What was its name? Infant . . . Infant Service Center . . . something like that. But I must get away from him. If I stayed here, he might prevail on me, and I would do something I could never forgive myself for.

We walked to the university together in the morning and parted as we usually did to go to our respective buildings.

"Are you going to see that doctor today? Don't come home and tell me you didn't have the time or some other tricky excuse."

I didn't know it then, but these were the last words my husband was to say to me for a long time, till after Freer's Cove was behind me, even if not forgotten. No, never forgotten. Swallowing hard, head down so that I did not even have a parting look at his fleshy, handsome face, I went to my morning class.

It was no use. The lecture hall was large, the professor far away on a platform, reading from notes. I stopped outlining the substance of his words. What could they mean to me now? Why was I even here?

Like a child, I let myself slip into a daydream of retribution. I was wearing chiffon, something gauzy, looking indescribably desirable, clasping to my side our baby, boy or girl? healthy, brilliant, while Jed pleaded with me to come back, it was a terrible mistake that he had never stopped regretting. But the dream held no satisfaction. I did not care anymore if he regretted losing us. I did not want to live with him, I did not want to go back to that sad bed in that dingy room that held only the death of love. It would not be revenge that would keep me from him if he wanted us now; it would be only because I did not want to be married to him.

I knew the professor was dismissing us from the crashing of folding chairs around me. I rose, too, and went down to the bookstore to buy the newspaper. I did it automatically as I did every morning, taking it out to Washington Square Park to read until it was time for my eleven o'clock class in medieval fiction. I stared blankly at the paper in my hand. This can't go on. Take a positive step then, do *something*.

Get a job. That was the first step to breaking away. I could do nothing without a job; my part-time work in the library could not support me. I turned to the want ads. But what could I do? I had just worked two months as a model, and that only in a small department store in Springfield. I had never learned shorthand—wasn't I going to be a teacher?—and could only peck at the typewriter. File clerk? Waitress? Where to start?

The pages of ads were strange and alarming. I would have to say I was pregnant; how long would they keep me? The small print blurred. It seemed hopeless. And then I remembered. Mrs. Blader had come into our kitchen to talk to my mother when she had come back from her first visit to the agency. *They take care of the mothers from the start,* she had said, *they even find them jobs for as long as they can work, and then they give them a home until they have their baby....*

If I went to the agency, maybe they would find me a job. Maybe this was the proper place to start. What was that name? Something with infant.

I walked over to the telephone booth on the corner and looked in the directory. Infant. Infant Adoption Services. That must be it. I looked at my watch. If I hurried, I could speak with them and still be back at the library by one. Still clutching my books, I took the bus uptown.

The Infant Adoption Services was in a building without a sign, a shabby brownstone off the park, plainly made over from a private house. A desk and a switchboard had been set into what was once the entry hall. A woman looked at me as I came in.

"May I help you?"

"I just—" Now that I confronted her, it was hard to say. "I—I would like to speak to someone about . . . adoption. I mean, I'm going to have a baby, and I would like—"

"Have a seat in there," she said gesturing. "Someone will be down to see you."

There was a small waiting room, furnished with leather

chairs and many magazines about babies and parents. Two other people were in the room, a man and a woman. Together? No, they sat apart from each other, each reading. I sat down on the sofa beside the woman.

Had I made myself clear to the receptionist? Maybe this wasn't the place to wait at all. Certainly the man wasn't here for the same purpose as I was, and the woman was plainly middle-aged. I fidgeted. Get up and ask the receptionist again. She would think me pushy and impatient. Just then a woman entered, looked around, and came straight toward me.

"May I have your name, please, and address?"

"Daisy Fr— Holland." I had been Daisy Freeman for nineteen years, Daisy Holland for only one, and sometimes when I was tense, I stumbled. I even stumbled over the address.

"Your name will be called shortly," she said, rising to go away.

I said hurriedly, "Excuse me, but I wanted to ask you—" I lowered my voice to a sibilant whisper which sounded piercingly loud in that small quiet room. "Am I in the right place? Do you find jobs for girls who . . . want to—" I stopped. The man had stopped turning the pages of a magazine, the woman had recrossed her legs; they could hear every word I said.

"Your interviewer will answer all your questions in a few minutes," she said, taking herself and her index card away.

I could feel my cheeks burning. I did not dare look around at the other two people in the room. They must guess all. They could not have helped overhearing my words to the receptionist when I came in, her desk was just outside, scarcely ten feet away, and now if there was still any question about why I was here, I had just supplied the answer.

A stout woman in tweeds came to the door with a card in her hand. "Mrs. Wilson?"

The woman sitting beside me followed her out.

I looked at my watch. The man would be next, then me. He had put down his magazine and got to his feet. Maybe he was tired of waiting, maybe he would leave and I could be next—

"Excuse me."

His gray worsted legs were directly in front of me. I looked up, startled, into his face.

How to describe that first impression? It is too bound up now with the months that followed, of knowing him, of being close to him, so that emotions are hard to separate. New England, I thought, icicles hanging from porch eaves. A fire in the hearth of a book-lined library. Tea on family silver. No, more. His narrow face was strict, uncompromising; his eyes fixed on me held something back, something troubling.

I had to pull my own eyes away. "Yes?"

"I wonder . . . could we talk? My name is Amos Freer."

I murmured doubt.

"There's a place on the corner that sells coffee. It would be more comfortable to talk there." He would not listen to doubt.

"I have to see someone, here."

"So do I. But this won't take long. I promise."

"I'm sorry. I haven't much time, and I must see—"

"Please." He smiled. It was an irresistible combination, that austere face and the smile that warmed it like a glow.

"You're here about a job, and I want to hire someone. Please."

So I found myself walking out with Amos Freer, past the curious glance of the receptionist, to a small sandwich shop on the corner. He left me at the table and went to the counter for our two cups of coffee.

"Now," he said, putting one in front of me, and the other opposite at his place, "let me explain fast why I brought you here, and if you're not interested, we can both get back to the agency for our interviews. You *are* looking for a job?"

I nodded.

"I assume . . . I mean, I did hear you say when you came in that you were going to have a baby. Is that true?"

I nodded again.

He smiled. "I have a job to offer you," he said. "It isn't as much of a coincidence as it might seem, actually. You came here to look for work until you could give up your baby for adoption. I came to engage a companion for my wife."

"But here? At the Infant Adoption Services?" I had finally found my voice.

"My wife is pregnant. We would like to have a companion for her who is also pregnant."

I stared hard, to see if he was serious.

"I know these agencies try to find work for the girls who come there. It isn't easy. Most employers won't keep on a girl once the pregnancy is well advanced, but that's our real point, you see. We'd like someone to stay till the end. You can't be far along, and neither is my wife, so it would be a job until the babies were born."

"I don't see—" My puzzlement must have shown on my face.

"If I've left things out, it's because they're personal," he said quietly. "You only need to know them if you take the job."

I suppose I just couldn't believe that my situation could be solved for me this simply. It was as if he had anticipated my every difficulty and eliminated them.

He misunderstood my hesitation. He said, "There'd be no physical work at all, outside of keeping my wife company. And you'd have a damn sight nicer place to live than what they could offer you here."

"I'm sure—"

"And no questions asked," he said meaningfully.

I guessed at once what he meant. I said with dignity, "I am married. My husband goes to law school. I'll get my BA at the end of the year, but we can't afford to have a baby right now, and so I'm looking for a job to support myself."

I was stunned to see the interest leave his face.

"I see," he said slowly. "I'm sorry. I didn't understand. I didn't think your situation was anything like that. After all, any girl that comes to an adoption agency would . . . I assumed—I'm sorry," he said again. "Of course I wouldn't think of separating husband and wife. This job would take you out of New York. To Maine, actually."

He put down his coffee cup and put a quarter under it. "I hope I haven't taken up too much of your time. If you hurry, I'm sure they'll see you."

Now it was my turn to be eager. In the few moments I'd had to think over his words I was beginning to realize how perfect an opportunity he had been offering me. And now was withdrawing. I too did not look forward to spending the last months waiting for the baby in a dormitory situation with a number of equally unhappy girls. He was offering a real home, and the easiest kind of work, and with what promised to be attractive people. I said quickly, "Actually, my husband and I are separating."

Was that a flicker in his eye? Disbelief? Interest?

But it was true. I would leave Jed the moment I felt I could support myself, and that moment was here. I went on, "We have been on the verge of separating even before. And he doesn't want the baby, and you see, I don't want to abort it. I mean, once it's born I plan to give it up, but I don't want to kill it, but . . . my husband insists on abortion." I do not enjoy gushing the most intimate facts of my life to strangers, but I guessed that the position depended on his knowing exactly how it was.

He continued to sit there, listening to me, so I had at least managed to revive his interest. I was puzzled by the expression on his face, his narrowed eyes studying me, until it came to me. He thought I was making it up! The husband, the separation—all invented to save face. But convincing him then was not as important as getting the job, and he seemed to prefer me without a husband.

I could see why, with his next words. "Your husband poses problems. Suppose you and he change your mind about the separation? Suppose he should want the baby after all? Wouldn't you pack up and return to him? I couldn't expect you to do otherwise. Anything else would be cruel and unnatural."

In a way he was sealing my option, making my decision irrevocable. Maybe he was only forcing me to clarify my own thinking, making me see what I had only half faced. I said firmly, "I will never go back to him under any circumstances."

"How can you be so sure?"

"I give you my word."

"Come now." He smiled, as if a word were useless under these circumstances.

I took the offensive. "Would it be so dreadful if I *were* to change my mind? You could always hire someone else."

"This is personal, too," he said. "And again, I'll explain if and when you come to take the job. All you have to know now is that it's essential you stay with us until our child is born."

"I will promise that."

"Suppose he comes after you."

"He won't," I said bitterly.

"Suppose he does. It wouldn't be inconceivable that he have a change of heart."

"How can he come after me," I said, "when I don't intend to tell him where I am?"

He repeated each word. "You don't intend to tell him where you are?"

I shook my head.

He said, "You might get lonely and write him. Maine can be a lonely place in winter."

So can New York, to a stranger. I was glad it was to be as far away as Maine. I wanted to put miles between Jed and me.

"Someone in your family might let the information slip, and he would find out."

I explained about my family. "My aunt and I exchange letters about twice a year and cards at Christmas."

He was playing with his coffee spoon, but something in his manner made me feel that I had turned the tide again in my favor. "What would you tell your husband if you were to see him before you left for Maine?"

"Only that I was leaving him. He wouldn't ask. Anyway, I don't have to see him. I could pack my things right now and spend tonight in a hotel."

"Or we could leave immediately," he said. "It takes less than nine hours on the new turnpike to where we live. I only came here to interview girls for the job. I've found her—" He smiled. "I don't like to leave my wife or the business for longer than I have to."

"I'll go and pack and be ready when you are!"

He said, "Suppose he comes in while you're packing."

"He never comes home before four. He has classes straight through until then."

"Would he cut, by some chance?"

"If he did, he wouldn't come home." What was there at home, to make him want to come there, except me, no lure to him?

"Then why don't you come with me while I check out of my hotel, and then I can drive you to your apartment for your things."

It's settled, I thought dazedly as we walked out of the coffee shop. I have left my husband, I have a job, I am going to have the baby. All due to the presence of this quiet man with a hint of steel, a hint of secrets, lurking in that shut-tered gray glance. As we got into the taxi I remembered suddenly that I hadn't even asked what my salary would be. Money was no longer that important now that I would have a home until the baby was born; still, I must act practically, Jed kept telling me that.

"How much does the job pay?" I tried to sound business-like.

He countered, "How much would you hope to get at any job you applied for?"

I stammered, "A hundred and twenty-five a week?"

He smiled. "But that would be without room and board." He watched me. "Will a hundred do?"

A hundred clear dollars every week. I was delighted.

We got out in front of the Lancaster. "You can wait in the lobby," he told me. "Or there's a writing room. You might want to leave your . . . your husband a note."

I hadn't thought of that; he saw it on my face.

He said, "After all, you can't just drop out of sight. He'll worry. Or maybe even set the police after you. It would be simpler to tell him you are going away."

I should have thought of it myself. Even if Jed didn't care a damn about me, he would feel obliged to act like a husband and trace me. I went into the writing room and using the creamy vellum of the Lancaster Hotel—that should set him speculating!—I wrote: "I am going to have the baby far from New York. Don't try to find me, because I have decided that it would be happier all around if we ended the marriage. I know we cannot afford to divorce now, but I have a job and will save the money so I can fly to Mexico once the baby is born. So you see this won't cost you any money or inconvenience. Daisy."

There was time to write two more notes: one to the library telling them that I must leave my job unexpectedly and to send any money coming to me in a check made out to Jed

Holland; the other to the university, letting them know I would not be back this year and, if a refund of tuition was possible, to send that to my husband, too. The checks would soften the blow of my leaving, I thought bitterly: Jed could always comfort himself with a new suit.

The car was waiting for us when Amos joined me. It was an expensive car, beautifully clean and polished but no longer new, witness to the same Yankee thrift, no doubt, that had made him cut down my salary request even when it couldn't have made any difference to him and, I sensed, he would have given me the amount I asked without any protest if I insisted.

He moved into the traffic. "You've written the note?" I said yes. "Sure you didn't forget and let him know where you're going?"

"Of course not!"

"People sometimes slip up on the small details. Tell me where you live and how to get there."

I directed him downtown. The streets narrowed, and there were garbage pails still littering the sidewalks, waiting to be picked up. The streets smelled of them, and of gasoline, and of heat. What must he think of my neighborhood? He said only, "You'll be better off, having your baby where we live."

I had to agree. But nevertheless, as we turned into our block a lump formed in my throat. Not because I would miss this ugly house with the cracked glass in the front door and the rusting iron stair rails, but because not so long ago I had dreamed of being happy here with Jed. What had it mattered, this shabby neighborhood, this cramped and dark apartment? We would be together. How quickly it had all gone! But would it have died so quickly, if it had ever truly lived?

And now, what was I leaping into, in my crazy, illogical way? I should have talked to Jed first; I should at least have told him of my plans.

It was Amos who touched my arm gently. "Can I help you? Can you manage by yourself?"

I nodded and got out hurriedly. I did not want him to come inside and see how I lived. I wasn't ashamed of the apartment, only that he would sense the death of love that lingered there like a sour odor.

I found the large leather valise that had been my father's and put in it the few clothes I had, my slacks and sweaters and boots and a ski suit that would come in handy in the cold of Maine, but for how long would I be able to wear them? I had to remind myself that now I would have money to buy what I needed. I didn't even have a warm coat, its purchase had loomed like an insurmountable hurdle up to now—but now there would be money for that, too. I had one pretty dinner dress that Jed had picked out for me when we were first married: I put that in.

I closed the straps of the valise and straightened up. The alarm clock—I would leave that; he had none. The pictures of my parents, I could slip them in my big pouch bag slung on my shoulder. My books—let him sell them. I looked around. It was as if I had never lived here. I remembered the note and propped it up on his pillow.

I looked back before I closed the door and uttered one small sound of anguish. But then I clamped my lips firmly and lifted my valise and went down the stairs for the last time.

Amos was waiting for me on the sidewalk and took my valise and put it beside his bag in the trunk. He helped me inside and shut the door firmly. The moment of anguish had passed. My decision was final. My baby would be born under the best of conditions, without anxiety, in a house in the country still unknown. Once he was given up for adoption I would have enough money saved together with my loan to help me finish school.

Now and then in the months to come the moments of anguish would return, but weaker, finally to become an illusion, even as the illusion of Freer's Cove would loom ever larger, and more real, until it became my life.

2

On that drive to Freer's Cove Amos asked me often if I thought I had accepted his offer too hastily, if I might have regretted it. He reminded me that there was still time to change my mind.

"I only have to drive you to the nearest bus station," he said. "I'll provide you with a return ticket, so at least you'll have had a pleasant ride in the country for your trouble."

But I had no thought of reversing my decision. He must have sensed that I was as anxious for the job as he was to have me. I know that if he had waited to be interviewed, there would have been other young women as eager for the job as I was, but somehow I felt intuitively that none might have proved as suitable. I did not know then what his wife, Joan, was like, but I could guess at the kind of girl he would have married, and he would be particular about whom he moved into his own house into the kind of enforced intimacy of the position. I was less than a year away from my degree. In spite of my long hair and fringes and chains, I think I still look as if I had been brought up properly, by old-fashioned standards.

And I do not think I would have accepted his job offer as quickly if I too had not been impressed. Not only by such old-fashioned virtues as substance and breeding, but as much by his look, by the suggestion of sadness behind the sternness, intensity behind the discipline. Fire and ice, a romantic combination to an impressionable girl, and I was always too much that.

I was not that overcome that it did not occur to me that in leaving to come with him I had burned my bridges, severed my ties with Jed and my former life so completely that I had left no trace of myself behind. If Amos Freer chose now to drive up some deserted road and rape and murder me, who would even link me with him? I should have been more uneasy, but I was not, though now and then I found myself glancing at him, as if for confirmation of my confidence, for reassurance.

He caught one of my covert glances.

"I promised to tell you—didn't I?—why it was important that you stay, why a husband could be a serious inconvenience. Are you troubled by that?"

"Well—"

"You may as well hear it now, all of it. You see, I'm not sure my wife could stand it if she should become attached to you and then you would leave her. She is in a rather emotional state now, one that isn't likely to get any better."

He turned his face briefly from the long green parkway on which we were traveling to see if he had alarmed me.

"There's been a tragedy in the family. Joan took it very hard." He was quiet, deliberating how much to tell me, I thought. "She needs someone she can depend on and trust entirely. Once she accepts you as her friend, it would be traumatic if you were to suddenly up and abandon her. So you see, go now if you've a mind to, but not later."

"I understand." My throat was dry. What had I let myself in for; how adequate would I be?

"Let me explain about the Freers. Things you should know. You've heard of Bright River Fisheries?"

It was hardly a question. How many cans of their fish had served as our hurried dinners?

"It belongs to the Freers."

I was impressed.

"It was my grandfather who started it, my father who built it up to what it is. There are three of us now, my sister, Frances, my brother, Ernest. My mother is dead. Ernest was the first to marry, then I, then Frances, and my father found himself alone in the house my grandfather had built. It was large, and he was lonely, and as he grew old and the business was not as important to him, he became increasingly anxious to have his family near him, and especially he loved the grandchildren. He made a proposition to us, or rather it was more of a mandate. He offered to build wings onto the house to provide each of us with separate apartments so that we should all live with him. He has become somewhat of a tyrant. He made it part of the inheritance structure."

All of this seemed to have nothing to do with Joan or the tragedy, and I found it hard to concentrate on what he was saying.

"My sister didn't mind. Actually, she even preferred it. Frances became very close to my father after my mother died. And it wasn't as if we didn't have privacy, as you will see. My father never intrudes on us. He's had two strokes and gets around in a wheelchair. There are family dinners once a week and on holidays, but we would come together anyway under these circumstances. And my father is happy when the children are near, and he can watch them playing. He even built a playground for them, in the back of the house, so he can look down on them from the terrace." He paused and frowned. "It was after Ronnie he had the second stroke, which crippled him."

I breathed, "After Ronnie?"

He said, "We live on an isolated part of the coast. Isolated, because hundreds of acres belong to us, and there is only our house on them. The children could be quite lonely, which is the reason for the extensive playground Father built. You know, sliding ponds, play forms, swings. All set in an authentic yew maze that our gardener planted. There is even a wishing well."

He paused again, and a pulse began throbbing in his cheek near his jaw. The wishing well?

"It wasn't a real well, naturally. Only about a foot of water at the bottom, so that the kids could lower the pails and bring a few drops up. But Ronnie was only three."

"Who is Ronnie?"

"Ernest and Julia's child. I don't see how she managed to climb up and fall in, but she was always too quick for us to keep up with, a pixie, a will-o'-the-wisp. She must have struck her head on the concrete bottom. We found her drowned."

I caught my breath sharply.

"It was terrible for all of us. There was my father's stroke, far more serious than the first. My brother's marriage broke up afterward. Maybe it would have anyway, Julia wasn't happy here, but that coupled with Ronnie—And then Ernest went into a terrible depression. He seems to be coming out of it now, but for a while he never spoke to any of us. But it's Joan that's my main concern. She took it very hard. She's fearful. For all the children, but naturally especially for our own."

"But it was an accident!"

"Don't you think we've stressed that, over and over again? I was almost drowned when I was ten. There's a small pond not far from the house that Ernest and I used to sneak off to when we were kids. It was forbidden to us without supervision, because people from town would come and fish through the ice in winter and leave holes in it, but we went out one night to skate when we should have been in bed— And my sister, Frances, swallowed a whole bottle of aspirin, the flavored kind. Accidents happen to children all the time. But there's no reasoning a person out of fear. She's got to see for herself that babies will continue to be born, and grow up, and—"

"And that's why I'm being taken to Freer's Cove," I said. "To show her that I'm not afraid to have my baby there."

He smiled his unexpected, unlikely smile. "Bright girl. I'm more and more convinced I was lucky to find you."

How could I fail to respond?

"Your job will be to act as you always do and hope Joan will copy your example. Just be yourself, and accept the situation normally. That doesn't sound too difficult, does it?"

"It seems like a job I would very much like to do."

36

He took one hand from the wheel to press mine. "Thanks."

I think I sensed then that it would not be too difficult, either, to like Amos Freer. In fact, it might be too damned easy.

"This baby of ours is very important to both of us," he said. "You see, she's had two miscarriages. We want her to have the best of conditions; we want nothing to upset her. I've even urged her to go away, but she won't. I can't leave the business, and she wants to be with me."

I knew how she felt.

"I promise you, Daisy, that your baby will be just as important to us. I realize these aren't the most ideal of conditions for you, but we'll do everything we can to make it up to you."

His patently sincere concern almost unnerved me. It was all I could do to keep myself from weeping on his shoulder. I needed kindness, and I needed friends. By the weird stroke of luck that brought us together it seemed as if I were to have both.

I went back to something that bothered me, as much to change the mood to one less filled with emotion, "Wasn't there anyone to watch Ronnie? After all, a child of three—"

"There was Amy, who works as nursemaid for Frances. She's been with Frances ever since Jeffrey was born, and now Frances has three. Ronnie was younger than Maggie— Margaret—but always tagged after her, so Amy just watched the four of them. As well as her own child, who plays with Jeffrey, although he's slightly older."

"And yet, with Amy there—"

"We don't like to talk about it. Amy almost went out of her mind. She's a good, conscientious girl, but she fell asleep.

It was summer. Frances had taken the older children somewhere. She just had the baby and Ronnie. My father had
built the maze partly to keep out the wind, which can get
strong, so it's always sheltered inside, and warm, and quiet.
She was lying on the grass playing with the baby, and she
just fell asleep. It could happen to the most conscientious of
us. How could we blame her?"

We stopped at the Massachusetts border for coffee and a
sandwich. I thought, how luxurious not to have to weigh
each penny, not to have to balance the cost of peanut butter
or hamburger! The sun here was no longer a weapon, but
just cheerful and warming, the air did not make my shirt
stick to my back. It blew my hair; it smelled sweet. I would
have liked to walk through the grove of trees behind the
roadside stand, to enjoy the first touches of yellow in the
branches, but Amos was anxious to get home in time for
dinner, and he steered me firmly back to the car.

He drove faster now and with great concentration, and
when he wasn't making conversation, his face would sink
back into that brooding, almost frowning preoccupation. I
wondered what he was thinking of. His wife, no doubt, and
the baby. What a pity that she should suffer from fear when
she didn't have to, when she had every ingredient for happiness, a loving husband, wealth, security, every ingredient
but couldn't realize it.

Autumn came closer as we drove north and east. By the
time we crossed into Maine at Kittery the sun had set, and
I rolled up my window against the sudden cold. I remembered again that I had no warm coat.

"Are there stores in Freer's Cove?"

"There is nothing in Freer's Cove but Freers." He smiled.
"The town of Bright River is ten miles away. That's where
our plant is. Do you drive?"

I had to admit that though I drove occasionally, we had
never had a car since my father died, and so I had never had
a license.

"It's no problem," he said. "Ernest and I and Walter, he's
Frances' husband, drive into Bright River every day. And
Frances and Joan both drive. They go into Portland to shop,
or even to Boston for anything important. Since we found
out about the baby, though, the doctor thinks it better that
Joan doesn't drive."

That reminded me. "I'll need a doctor."

"We have a very good doctor, Dr. Raab. He's always
within call for the family. Joan only visits the specialist in
New York because of the trouble she's had. You'll like
Raab."

As fast as a problem arose, it was smoothed away. I put
my head back on the seat and closed my eyes. I went over in
my mind what I had written to Jed. I wondered if he would
care, even a little. All I could imagine was that he would
breathe a great sigh of relief. My throat swelled. Amos must
not see me cry; I turned my head away, feigning sleep. But
I didn't cry, mainly I think out of pride. I too could breathe
a great sigh of relief; I too would be rid of an embarrassing
mistake.

The road spun endlessly through evergreen forests; I
watched through half-closed lids. It grew very cold. Amos
put on the heater, and in the enveloping warmth I fell truly
asleep. It was our stopping that waked me.

Before my sleep-dazed eyes loomed tall iron gates, a stone

wall, trees behind trees. The gates were opening; we rolled inside and stopped again. Our headlights shone on a stooped old man dressed in a leather windbreaker and cap.

"Evening, Cory."

"Evening, Mr. Freer. Didn't expect you back this soon."

"I had a lucky break. How are things at the house?"

Cory hesitated. He had discovered me at Amos' side and peered at me uncertainly.

Amos followed his look and saw that I was awake. "Daisy, this is Cory, our gardener. Cory, this is Daisy Holland, who is going to be with us for a while."

Cory touched his cap, and then came close to the window. "Been some excitement, Mr. Freer. Family thinks it was my doing, carelessness, but I don't leave such stuff around where the children can get at 'em—"

"*What happened?*" There was alarm under the peremptoriness.

"The baby drank some of that pesticide stuff. She found the bottle where I'd been working, but I'd never—"

"My God," said Amos thinly. "How is she?"

"Fine now. Been to the hospital in Portland, but they say she'd only taken a drop. They shouldn't blame me, Mr. Freer—"

"All right, Cory. We better get on to the house."

The car shot forward through borders of laurel and rhododendron. I wondered at the look on his face now that he knew the baby was out of danger, and I questioned him. "But if she's fine now—"

"Don't you understand?" he said with unexpected shortness. "Joan will be frightened. She'll interpret this as she did Ronnie's death."

A thin section of orange moon hung low but shed little light. Only our headlights pierced the black tunnel of branches. Without warning a great clearing opened suddenly in front of us. In the center of it sat the house, three-storied and square, its two wings supporting it like buttresses. It was cupolaed and turreted and dormered and chimneyed, which almost hid the pure plain shape of the original house and gave it an air of fantasy. We circled the great arc of driveway. Lights shone in many downstairs windows.

"If we hurry," Amos said, "we can still catch them at dinner, and you can meet everyone at once." He made a wry face.

He came around to help me out and up shallow granite steps. The door was opened promptly to his ring. A man peered at us and then stepped aside to let us in. He echoed Cory's words.

"We didn't expect you back this soon, Mr. Freer."

"I had a stroke of good luck. The family still in the dining room, Sam?"

Sam nodded. "Shall I have two more places set?" He was scrutinizing me under heavy brows.

"Yes, please. Sam, this is Daisy Holland, who's going to stay with Joan. Sam, who takes care of my father."

I smiled, he nodded.

"There's luggage in the car, Sam. And will you show Daisy where she can wash up before we go in?"

Amos went upstairs, I was taken by Sam to a large powder room off the hall. There were marble basins and a long gilt mirror, scented soaps in crystal jars, and a profusion of thick towels. All at once I felt dusty and out of place. I had moved into another life, one I had only read about, the world of the rich. I combed my hair smooth and took off all but one jingling belt, burying the rest in my handbag.

When I came out, I had only a moment to glimpse the vista of the wide staircase, separating into two at the landing, of the brass and crystal chandelier that hung above it, lighting the dark wood that paneled the hall. Amos was coming down the stairs toward me. He took my arm and pushed open the double doors.

Five faces stared at us from around the long damask-covered table, startled for an instant into silence. Then the exclamations began, and the explanations. A slight figure of a girl had risen at once and came running to Amos, putting her arm through his. They kissed, and then he turned to me, still holding her arm.

"This is Daisy Holland. Joan, my wife."

"Welcome," she said, and put a small, cold hand in mine.

"My father," said Amos, gesturing at the old man who sat in a wheelchair at the head of the table. "My sister, Frances. My brother-in-law, Walter. My brother, Ernest."

I was aware of a servant busy laying plates and napkins, but the faces had blurred into the shadows of the room, and I did not even try to distinguish them.

"Sit here, Miss Holland," said Frances, gesturing at the place beside her. "Let me help you to some wine."

"First, how is Moira?" said Amos, sitting down beside Joan. "Cory told us when he let us in."

"Cory is getting old and forgetful," said Frances thinly.

"Moira is good as new, Amos. She should be outside playing in the morning." This must be Walter. His face was bland, large.

"We weren't that sure of her this morning," Frances said, cutting into the meat on her plate.

I felt eyes on me. I finally allowed myself to lift my head, and looked into a face vaguely resembling Amos', but so different, brown-bearded and with angry eyes. They stared at me hostilely.

This must be Ernest.

3

I had lost the sense of place. I had no clear concept of where we were except as a dot on a vast green place that was the state of Maine. Compounding the displacement, adding to the effect of warmth and food and wine after the long cold drive, was the drastic change my life had taken. No wonder that first dinner at the Freers' was a series of distorted images and faces.

Dazedly I felt I were in some movie version of an English manor house. There was all that dark paneling, the drawn draperies, the white uniformed maid and Sam in his dark jacket moving about silently, lifting plates, filling glasses. I felt that when the picture was over I would be walking out on the streets of Greenwich Village, back to the apartment on Tenth Street. I remember the appraising looks of Frances and her husband and the blank stare of Mr. Freer, wondering who I was. But especially I remember the cold, hostile eyes of Ernest.

Mr. Freer's stroke had affected his speech. When he managed to say a few words, it was with great difficulty, and all of us waited, struggling silently with him, until he had got them out. Joan whispered to me that he would not have therapy; he was too weak for the effort required. He managed to convey to me across the table that I was too thin, that I needed more flesh to withstand the Maine winter. Frances had to interpret for me. She said briskly, "Daddy, we'll have to explain to Miss Holland what a tease you are."

A polite rumble came from Walter's throat. To this day I cannot clearly evoke an image of Walter except that he was large and pale and in the middle of his face were those glinting, gold-rimmed glasses. Frances, on the other hand, was, and is, distinct, her heavyset golfer's shoulders, her legs planted squarely when she stood, her dress dowdy and made to last for years, her hair cut with a mannish shingle in the back, her skin ruddy and weathered, more so than her brothers'. It was impossible to imagine Walter and Frances finding each other attractive enough to marry, let alone to produce three children, but then my conception of love was still romantic. That night with my eyes heavy and dry, my cheeks burning, the room pulsing, my inner confusion was compounded by pictures of Walter and Frances like two gray whales meeting and joining under the ocean.

Coffee was served in the library, adjoining the dining room. The scenario continued as we moved into a book-lined room where a fire burned in a large stone hearth. We formed into groups, Amos and Walter talking business, Joan beside me, Frances hovering over her father. Only Ernest moved off alone, his back turned to the room and us.

The room was too dark, the corners too shadowy. Conversation was muffled, and the only clear sound was the chiming of silver and china as our coffee was poured by Sam.

There was scarcely light to see clearly, let alone read, yet Ernest took down a book and went to sit near the fire with it, as if reading were a pretext to shut himself away from everyone.

"Why won't you turn on more lamps?" I whispered to Joan.

"My father-in-law prefers it this way," she said. "He's had cataracts removed from his eyes, and bright areas of light give him a headache."

We regrouped, and I found myself momentarily alone. Walter noticed, and refilled my empty cup, and sat down beside me.

To make conversation I said, "You must have had a terrible fright, with Moira."

He darted a quick look at Mr. Freer, to make sure he was out of hearing range, and then said in a low voice, "We don't want Father or Joan upset, so we are making light of it. Not that we believe it was deliberate, nothing like that, of course," he said with a hearty laugh, but almost as if he were denying a doubt in his own mind. "The pesticide was lying under some flowers where Cory had been using it, and it was natural for the baby to pick it up and put to to her mouth. It was in a glass ketchup bottle."

I looked surprised.

"Cory has been doing that for years. He keeps empty bottles for that reason. He mixes up a pail of insecticide and then pours it into small bottles that he can carry in his pocket. He was working over some plants in the maze, and he just left it there by mistake, I suppose."

Frances had moved over to us. "The less said about it in

front of Father or Joan, the better. I hope you told Cory off properly, Walter."

"I did. I told him one more mistake like that and he's through."

"He said he's always careful of such things," I said.

"He always is," Frances said. "It's not like him at all. But he is getting old. Luckily Amy saw Moira pick it up and recognized it as one of Corey's bottles. We got her to vomit even before Dr. Raab came, and probably it wasn't even necessary to bring her to the hospital."

"She wouldn't have wanted to swallow much, after the first taste," I said.

"Still, she might have," Frances said. "I keep thinking, suppose Amy hadn't seen her. We might have assumed it was an ordinary stomachache and not even called Raab."

There was a silence. Walter said uncomfortably, "I suppose Amos told you about Ronnie, Miss Holland."

I nodded.

"Ever since Ronnie, you could say we're all overreacting," Walter said. "Maybe Joan has infected us, but we're all too prone to see sinister aspects to perfectly normal happenings. Joan will tell you that there's a kind of doom or curse hanging over the children, and my usually sensible wife is beginning to wonder, especially after today."

"I don't believe in a doom or a curse," Frances said flatly. "You're being ridiculous, Walter. It's nothing as mysterious or supernatural as that. But I can't help wondering." She stopped.

Walter interposed smoothly, "Anyway, don't you think we've filled Miss Holland with enough nonsense for one night? What kind of family will she think she has elected to stay with? You mustn't brand us as neurotics, Miss Holland, no matter how we sound today. It's just that we're still a bit shaken."

"I'm not surprised," I said. "I'd feel the same way if it was my child, following so close on . . . on that other accident. And won't you call me Daisy? Besides, I'm not Miss Holland, actually, but Mrs. Holland."

Frances said, "I'm sorry. I thought Amos introduced you as Miss Holland."

"I hope not. I am not only married, but I'm going to have a baby."

They both stared.

"You don't look old enough," said Walter heartily.

"You can't be very far along," said Frances.

I shook my head.

"Joan has just started a baby, too."

"Amos told me."

Walter laughed. "When Amos told us he'd try to find someone to keep Joan company who was also going to have a baby, it seemed like a rather farfetched notion. We never thought he'd bring it off. But you can't underestimate Amos."

"Amos is like my father," said Frances. "He's tenacious. And cool. And brainy. I admire Amos' brain; I always have. I think you will be very good for Joan, you seem so healthy and uncomplicated, Miss . . . I mean Mrs. . . . . No, Daisy, of course." She looked flustered, and remembering that I was married, the inevitable thought came to her: "Where is your husband?"

"Come now, Frances," said Walter. "That's none of your business."

"It's all right." I was beginning to expect the question. "My husband and I are separated."

The quick glance that flashed between them said: is there a husband? and answered: probably not. Maybe I had just grown too sensitive to the situation, but I could understand their logic. Mothers-to-be, when married, are usually found at their husbands' sides.

Frances had tactfully changed the subject. "Joan is such a delicate girl. I sometimes wonder how she will manage to carry a baby all the way."

I wondered myself, looking at Joan.

"She would have gone to California to have her baby at her father's house, except that she adores Amos and won't leave him for a day. And yet she is so nervous now, so moody. It's sad. They've wanted a child for years, they've tried unsuccessfully twice, you know, and now that she is finally embarked on this third one it has to be spoiled by fear."

"But she has Daisy to stay with her, and maybe you'll have a healthy effect on her, Daisy. She was once fine, remember, before Ronnie's accident, and maybe she'll get back to her old self again now. Frances," Walter said, "how about bed? I for one am ready."

But Frances went on, almost as if she hadn't heard. "This hasn't exactly been a cheerful house, for many years. Mother's illness, and then Father's strokes. Ronnie. Ernest's trouble with Julia, and then Julia just up and disappearing, not a note, not a trace. Ernest doesn't speak to us since Ronnie died. It's as if he blamed us for what happened. Sometimes I feel positive hatred in his look—"

Walter stood up. "I do think we ought to go to bed this minute, Frances. Didn't you want to look in on Moira?" He took her firmly by the elbow.

She stood up, too, and tried to laugh. "You must forgive us for sounding off tonight, Daisy. We'll say good-night. You look as if you could use some shut-eye yourself."

I would have liked nothing better than to go off to bed, but I didn't feel free to suggest it to Joan. I watched them make their good-nights, Frances lingering with her father while Walter stood impatiently in the door waiting for her. Amos and Joan continued to sit beside Mr. Freer. My eyes were closing from fatigue. Some more coffee might keep me awake. I half rose to get some from the table when Ernest stood up.

"Would you like some coffee?"

I was surprised that he had noticed my move. I gave him my cup and took it back from him filled. He continued to stand over me. I tried to think of something to say, but no words would come. His unfriendliness chilled me.

He said, "Why should you want to come here?"

I was taken aback and faltered. "I was offered a job."

"Why here?"

I met his eyes almost defiantly. "But why not?"

He didn't answer. He didn't move away. He continued to stare at me, brooding. In the same abrupt way he said, "Have you known Amos long?"

"We met only today. At the—" I hesitated. "At the agency."

"What a lucky break for both of you," he said softly. "That you each found what you were looking for."

I told myself: He is ill. He is equally hostile to the others in the family. I must excuse him, overlook his rudeness. I said, "It *was* a lucky break. Amos and I both thought so."

He said, "Why should someone who seems as intelligent as you be willing to take a menial job like companion?"

I could feel the blood rush to my face. "I don't consider it menial. If you overheard any of our conversation before, you must know I'm going to have a baby, and there aren't many jobs that I could keep to the very end. I happen to need the money."

I got to my feet and put my untouched coffee cup down on the table and went over to where Joan sat. She looked surprised at my sudden appearance and then conscience-stricken.

"Daisy, we've been so inconsiderate, making you stay up when you're tired."

"I am, a little." And bruised by my encounter with your brother-in-law. And beginning to wonder if I shouldn't have thought the job over for at least another day.

"It's time for bed for all of us," Amos said. "Sam?"

Sam reappeared from somewhere and, unfastening the brake on Mr. Freer's chair, wheeled him out into the hall. We followed. Sam pressed a button, and a section of paneling opened in the wall revealing a small elevator. Sam pushed the wheelchair inside.

"Good night!" we called.

But Mr. Freer's head was already sunk on his chest, his eyes closed.

"It's the medicine he takes," Joan said. "It keeps him sedated most of the time."

We climbed the steps to the floor above, pausing on the

landing as Sam and Mr. Freer and the wheelchair all vanished behind double doors. There were two other sets of double doors on the landing; Amos pointed to the pair on the right.

"That's Frances and Walter's apartment. Ernest's is below it. This is where we live."

He held the doors open for Joan and me. I went in and stopped, astonished. I was in the foyer of what appeared to be a complete small house, entirely out of character with the big one that contained it. It was as charming as a doll's house. The furniture was pine and cherry, the wallpaper covered with bouquets, the rugs hooked in bright patterns, pitchers and baskets of fresh flowers everywhere.

"It's like our house in California," Joan said, in response to my surprise. "Amos said I could do it that way if it would make me happier here."

"Show it to her in the morning," said her husband. "What Daisy wants to see most right now is her bed."

Joan took me down the hall to my room. It had a window seat, and white wainscoting, and flower-sprigged paper, and a four-poster bed. Ruffled drapes hung at the casement windows. I ran to them to look out.

There was a broad lawn, on which the lighted windows below threw an amber pattern. As I looked, the lights were turned out, and the scene restored to night. I began to make out the pattern of darker yews. This must be the maze, the playground where Ronnie—

I cried out. A wickedly gleaming Halloween face hung below. In an instant it vanished.

"What is it?" Joan was beside me.

I made myself laugh. "I don't know." And then the

branches parted again, and there was the face, not as frightening this time.

"That's the sliding pond," she said. "It does have an awful face. But the children adore it."

I could partly make it out now; the chute was set into a wrought-iron frame molded to look like a Halloween witch, complete to peaked hat, her gleaming eyes and wicked toothless grin picked out with a kind of phosphorescent paint. When the wind parted the branches, the face hung, revealed.

Joan said faintly, "I thought you saw the wishing well. It's there, see, in the heart of the maze. See the roof?"

We both looked down on it in silence.

She said, "Someone left the poison there deliberately, for the baby to drink."

"Joan, even Frances says it must have been Cory."

"Let her think what she wants." She turned away. She said, "I don't like it here, Daisy. I don't like to look at the maze. I wish we could go away."

"Why don't you, then? A short holiday would be good for you."

"I can't leave Amos," she said. "He needs me."

I thought pityingly: But you need him more. I drew her away from the night outside and the witch's face and that well where a child had drowned, back into the flowering bower of a room.

"Joan, this is the prettiest room I've ever seen."

"But I can't shut out the house, no matter what I do. It's an unhappy house. Terrible things have happened here."

"Terrible things happen everywhere. In cities, too."

She shook her head. She said in a low voice, "I'm afraid of sickness. Father. Ernest."

"Have you told Amos how you feel?"

"Yes, but what can he do? Father made it so that we can't live anywhere else. Amos doesn't want to. Leave Frances alone with Father? She's done enough harm already—"

"Harm—"

Amos' voice called from the hall, "Can't you save the talk for tomorrow, Joan? You'll have months to fill her in on everything."

She moved toward the door at once. But she hesitated, and then in a light whisper she blurted out, "Go away, Daisy! Don't stay!"

She slipped out.

I closed the door after her. I must admit that her words disturbed me. I stared at my valise already opened on an embroidered luggage rack, at my pajamas on the pillow and my slippers below the bed. I had an impulse to lie in my clothes until morning, as if clothing made one less vulnerable to danger, and then in the morning to ask to be driven to the railroad station. Joan would lend me the price of the fare; she had urged me to go away; she would help me—

There was a tap on the door. I went to open it.

Amos stood there, in a dark robe over pajamas. He said, "Have you everything you need? Joan sometimes forgets to ask."

"Everything. Thanks."

He studied my face. "You mustn't let yourself be upset by Joan. Remember, that's why you're here. To help her."

I unconsciously clasped my hands together, to help myself be silent. He put his hands out and took my clasped hands in his.

"It's going to be all right now, Daisy, with you here. I promise you you won't regret it."

How can I explain the effect of his words, of his touch? There was something so sad in his eyes that it was I who wanted to reassure him.

"Don't worry about me, Amos. I'm sure I won't regret it."

A final pressure of his hands, and he said good-night. I took a shower in my own pink and white bathroom and climbed beneath a rose-patterned quilt. The comfort was pervasive. The well, the maze, the bottle of poison, the blackness outside, the unhappiness within, the entire state of Maine could not dispel the deliciousness of settling deep into sleep.

II

⚘

⚘

⚘

1

I WAKENED TO THE SOUNDS of children. They must be outside, in the street. Too-brilliant sunlight dazzled my eyes: I had forgotten to draw the blinds last night. The sunlight was that intense light found only near water. I was in a strange room, the bedroom of a doll's house. Where—I remembered, slowly.

The room was filled with an almost summery warmth. I went to the windows to push them out. Now I could see the maze clearly, thick, smoothly clipped, green-black yews making an ornate pattern. The pointed red roof of the wishing well looked cheerful enough in the morning sun; the tall witch was insubstantial, an arrangement of bars. I could see the red hair of some young woman moving within the maze, but the children were hidden.

Something shimmered, beyond. The ocean! Freer's Cove was beside the ocean!

I had surmised the ocean was near, it was that kind of light, but I hadn't guessed it was that close. Now I could smell it, that smell different from land smells, sharp, crisp. My heart lifted up. I was born inland, in Illinois, but I had always had this pull toward the sea, and one of the delights of living in New York to me had been that the ocean was close. Every chance I could find, we went to Jones Beach . . . that summer . . . Jed.

No, I would not let it spoil my mood. Was it too late for swimming? Amos had said the days were still warm. I dressed in a hurry, noting as I strapped on my watch that it was already ten o'clock. I was hungry. I found the small dining room easily, and Joan in it, still having her own breakfast, wearing quilted silk with lace at the neck. She looked like a doll in her own dollhouse, seated on a yellow velvet seat on a lyreback chair. The draperies were yellow chintz, the wallpaper striped yellow and brown.

"How you must have enjoyed decorating this house!"

She said, "We were happy then. That was before."

Before what? Ronnie? Change the subject. "It isn't like me to sleep this late."

"I never get up early. What for?"

"How luxurious!" I was determined not to notice her dejection. Still, she did not talk about my leaving: Had Amos spoken to her, or did the house seem different to her, too, in the morning? How luxurious, indeed, I thought again, as a middle-aged woman in an apron over her cotton dress brought in a tray with orange juice and eggs and bacon. The coffeepot was on the table, with a silver rack of toast.

"Minna, this is Daisy Holland. Minna knows all about you."

We said hello and smiled.

"Anything else you like, I can fix it for you," said **Minna**.

"This is more than I ever eat. Just toast and juice from now on, please, or I'll get fat."

"Don't look as if you ever could, any more than Joan here," said Minna, returning to the kitchen.

"Is there swimming, Joan? I'd love to go swimming."

She shivered at the thought. "Even in July it's cold for swimming, to me. And we have no beach here, only rocks, so you must be a good swimmer. There's the pond, but it's cold by this time of year. Too cold."

"Then let's at least walk down to the ocean. I'd love to see it."

"I don't like to walk there. It's all cliffs—"

"Please come, Joan. It'll be good for you."

She looked doubtful but agreed.

"Didn't your obstetrician tell you that exercise is good for you?"

She said, "I don't think there's anything that will help me."

"That's a dreadful thing to say! You can't mean it!"

But I could understand her words. She seemed lost inside that quilted robe, too fragile, her skin transparent, blue-veined, those child's wrists. How could she sustain the weight of a baby?

She went in to dress while I finished a second cup of coffee. I carried my dishes in to Minna, feeling a twinge of guilt. Nothing to do, no dishes to wash, till April!

When I followed Joan out of the small house into the large, it was almost a shock—I had been able so completely to put it out of mind. We went down the stairs and through glass doors to a stone terrace. Mr. Freer was folded into his blanket on his chair as if he were on the deck of a ship. We stopped to say good morning.

"He is always out here whenever the children are," she said. "It's almost as if he were guarding them."

"You give the most natural habit an ominous twist," I said, laughing at her.

"I sometimes wonder if he didn't see . . . Ronnie, see what happened to her," she said quietly. "He had the second stroke that night."

"Could he have seen into the maze from the terrace?"

"Easily. You see, it's much higher. And he used to have binoculars. They're too heavy for him to handle now, with one hand. But he still seems to see enough without them."

We were heading across the lawn, skirting the maze, when I said, "I'd love to see the children."

I might have guessed she did not want to go near the maze. Her mouth tightened, but she said only, "Of course. I should have thought of it myself." She led me back and around the green yew hedge until we found the narrow opening.

I was fascinated. "Is this the only way in?"

"There's another way. You're supposed to trace your way from one opening to the other. The children know all the paths easily by now."

Inside the maze I could see why it was an ideal playground for children. The wind, strong here, was entirely kept out, and the sun would beat down warmly. I had to shed my sweater and knot it around my waist. We came into a square clearing where chrysanthemums still blossomed, and there was the red-haired young woman I had glimpsed from my window, lying on the grass, a round-faced child of about a year lying on the blanket beside her.

Amy sat up at once when she saw us. "Morning, Mrs. Freer."

"Amy, this is Daisy Holland. Daisy is going to stay with us until I have my baby."

"Hi."

We inspected each other. She was not pretty, except for that fiery hair; her bones were too gaunt, her mouth too pinched.

"This is Moira," I said, kneeling beside the baby. She let me touch her silky round head, staring at me solemnly, and then she was caught by my gold bangle, and reached out a small curled hand to touch it. Her cheeks were still pale, from yesterday's experience. I thought of my own baby, round, silken, with those tiny curled fingers. . . .

"The kids are in there somewhere," Amy said. The dense thicket made them invisible, even though their voices were close. "Maggy? Jeff? Sandy?"

They materialized one behind the other, slowing down when they saw me, looking at me gravely. Maggie was the first to come forward. Square, stocky, she put her hand in mine and smiled at me out of Frances' eyes. "Who are you?"

"I'm Daisy. I'm going to stay with Aunt Joan for a while."

"This is Jeffrey," said Joan, and brought him forward almost protectively. He was thin, with a heavy thatch of dark hair spilling over his forehead and knobby knees. He put out his hand shyly to shake mine; it was plain he was being taught how to be a gentleman and a Freer.

"The big one is Sandy," said Amy, but proudly. "He's mine."

Sandy stood foursquare, his eyes sparkling and untroubled. Jeff seemed to watch his every move with admiration.

Sandy said, "You look like my kindergarten teacher."

"What's her name?" I asked.

"Miss Graham. We call her Crackers."

He burst into laughter, Jeff joining in delightedly.

"Sandy only goes to kindergarten afternoons," Amy said. "So he and Jeff can play together."

Jeff blurted out, "Next year I'm going to school with Sandy."

"Next year I'll be going in the morning for all day," Sandy said. "You'll only go afternoons with the kindergarten kids."

Jeff flushed and looked down. I had to suppress an instinctive move to pull him against me. "But the year after that you'll be going with the big boys, Jeff." He had the gentle look of a baby deer.

He said in a low voice to me, "Want to see the house Sandy and I are making?"

"I'd love to."

He put a grubby hand in mine and led me into the maze. Sandy darted ahead, Maggie trailed stolidly after. As we passed the wishing well, he hesitated. He said, "Ronnie got drowned in there."

But the other children had gone on, the tragedy forgotten, and were waiting for us in the center of the maze. They had found a refrigerator carton and surrounded it with branches, even to its roof. I admired it, and peered inside, where there was a tiny table with dishes on it. But Maggie was tugging me to the witch sliding pond, showing me how she climbed up and slid down. There was a jungle gym and concrete play forms of all kinds, and I had to admire them all, before I could say, "I'm lost. Who's going to take me back to Aunt Joan?"

All three did, delighted at my helplessness.

I said to Amy, "Your Sandy is a fine boy."

"Looks more than six, don't he?" she said proudly. "Everyone takes him for eight. He's handy, too. And sharp. He's the man of the house."

Sandy's fair skin reddened with pleasure.

We left them, Joan and I, continuing our walk. As we cut across the lawn, I said, "It's hard to imagine Amy doing anything as irresponsible as falling asleep when she's watching the children. She seems too alert, too sharp."

"She always is. That's why it's so hard to understand. That particular day she had only Ronnie and the baby to watch, because Frances took the other children into Bright River, and it was quieter than usual, and—"

"Maybe that was it," I said. "It was quiet, and she didn't have to have eyes in a dozen places at once, and she might have relaxed . . . lay down on the grass with Moira, like today—"

"Still, it isn't like Amy," she said stubbornly. "Amy has always been extra-conscientious, out of gratitude, I think. Sandy's father was a soldier at the base near here. He left without marrying her. She'd worked here as a maid, and Frances kept her on and let her keep Sandy, too. That's why she's so devoted, why she took it so hard. She wanted to leave, she was so ashamed, but we insisted. Even Ernest insisted."

The salt smell was stronger, but the ocean was still hidden from view. We skirted stables and sheds and a barn and cut past an extensive truck garden, with tall dried stalks of corn tied together. The grass was thick and yellow here, laced with wild aster. I was responsible for bringing the talk around to Ronnie, and I tried hard to make her forget it. I said, "Isn't it just like summer, the grass smells so hot and fragrant?" I said, "Look how milky pale the sky is!" but her face was shut away.

She said, "We wondered how Ronnie climbed to the top of the well. She was such a tiny thing, half Maggie's size."

"Was there something to stand on near it? A box?"

"Cory had left some empty seedling boxes around," she said dubiously.

"There. You see?"

But she only shook her head.

Now just a faded red snow fence separated us from the cliffs, from the hard-trodden narrow path that rimmed them. We searched for a place where the snow fence had been buffeted to the ground and stepped across it. There it was, a glittering ocean. My heart cramped at its vastness, its surface smooth as watered silk.

"I'm going to love it here!" I cried in my excitement.

"Be careful," she said nervously.

The path was narrow, and in some places the earth and rock had given way and it was only wide enough to allow one person to walk. We went one behind the other. Here was a place where a handrail of pipe had been hammered into the cliff side, and steps of stone set in roughly. They went down halfway and stopped at a wide ledge.

"Coming?" I had started down.

She shook her head. "Please don't go down, Daisy."

"But it's easy. And I do want to get down to the water, just once."

"The rocks are slippery. The spray washes over."

"I'm surefooted. And I'm wearing sneakers. Besides, the rocks ought to be dry in this sun. You stay there, then, and I'll be back up in a minute."

It was still a distance to the water from the ledge, and only a stone here and there to set one's foot on. I slid down from stone to stone, clutching at the dry scrubby plants that grew out of the cliff side. Heights do not bother me, and the prospect was intoxicating. The smell of seaweed grew stronger, acrid and briny. Mussels clung to the rock sides like shiny black beetles, washed by foam. I was down at last to the water's edge; the ocean rushed in hissing and swirling, retreating in white bubbles. I stooped to scoop up some water and felt my face sting with salt spray. I would have liked to stretch out on a flat rock in the sun, but Joan was there, peering down anxiously from above. . . .

And where was the sun?

The air had become a thick, pearly gray. In my concentration I had scarcely noticed that the clarity and warmth of the air had undergone a change.

Joan was calling, her voice thin and far away. She was pointing.

I followed the line of her arm. The sea was still clear. I could even see a tiny ship with the superstructure of a trawler making its way slowly across its surface. But just where she pointed the fog was coming in as if someone were unrolling thick batting. Shreds drifted past my face. The light was dull, the air like fine rain. I shivered.

"Daisy, hurry!"

Joan's voice was shriller.

I began my ascent, clutching, sliding back, digging my toes in, my heart pumping heavily. It seemed an age before I reached the safety of the ledge, but the rocks steps were oily now, and I clung to the wet pipe rail until I reached the path.

"You see why it's dangerous?" she scolded. "Even in summer the fog comes up suddenly. None of us walks here, except Ernest."

Fog swirled and eddied around the big house like smoke as we neared it, now hiding a chimney entirely, now a dormer. Far below a fog horn began to moan, punctuated by the constant thin tinkle of buoy bells. I shivered again, and Joan saw me.

"You should wear a heavy jacket when you go out this time of year."

"I must buy one, first chance you go shopping," I said, shoving my hands deep into the body of my sweater.

"We can go whenever you want."

But I had no money until I was paid for my first week here, and so I would have to wait.

"You might fit into some of Julia's things," said Joan, studying me as she walked behind me. "She left closets full of clothes. Ernest threw everything into cartons to be taken away, but Frances couldn't stand that. Frances is very thrifty. When Ernest was away, she saved everything and hung them in the storage closets. Ernest would be furious if he knew."

"Why should he care?"

"I suppose he didn't want anything belonging to Julia left, to remind him. And he wouldn't want Frances to touch her clothes. He hates Frances. But then since he got sick, he hates us all."

"I wouldn't want to wear anything of hers."

"A coat? A coat is . . . impersonal. It might not even have to be altered. Your figure is like Julia's. In fact, there is quite a resemblance. Not her features or her expression, but the way she walked, the way she carried herself."

"Why did she leave him, really?" I said. We were skirting the outbuildings now, the ocean behind us.

She hesitated. "Oh, there was plenty of talk, for miles around, I'm sure. Everyone could think of reasons. There were lots of them. The simplest is that she didn't love Ernest, that she married him to get out of Bright River, and now that she had money, why stay? I know she hated it here. She loved excitement and exciting places. Maybe she only stayed as long as she did because of Ronnie. Then there was no more reason." She paused. "And there was Frances."

"Frances?"

"Frances looked down on Julia."

"Why?" I caught myself. "Am I prying?"

"She's gone now, and it doesn't matter, I suppose," she said slowly. "Frances was furious when Ernest married her. Julia's father worked on one of our boats. He was Portuguese. Julia was beautiful. You could see why Ernest fell in love with her. I think Julia believed she could get Ernest away from Freer's Cove, and then Father made it part of the will that we live here while he lived, and she was trapped. Amos believes Frances engineered that clause, hoping to drive Ernest and Julia away."

I looked as shocked as I felt.

She saw my expression. "Frances can get Father to do anything she wants. After Mrs. Freer died, Father depended on Frances for everything. She has always schemed to take over the business. And Amos says if she had been a man, he's sure Father would have made her president of the company. The only thing that ever stopped him was his feeling that it was a man's business. So Frances uses other methods."

I hadn't noticed we had reached the house by another way from the way we had left, across the lawn and past the maze. We skirted the kitchen entry and entered the house through french doors that led into a long empty room, mirrored, with small gilt chairs lining the wall. It was cold. Joan said it was never used anymore and was left unheated, but when the Freer children were growing up, it had been used for parties, it was the ballroom, until Ann—

"Ann?" I had not heard this name before.

"Ann was the fourth child, the youngest. She was out riding when she struck her head on a branch and was killed at once. My mother-in-law never recovered from the shock. She was still ill when we were married and never even came to the wedding."

It did seem as if the Freers were star-crossed. And yet they were a large family, and the possibility of accident was multiplied. But it gave one pause: Even if Joan had not been as neurotic as she was, I could understand her apprehension for her unborn child.

2

We were back in the large paneled hall. We started for the staircase when halfway up we met Frances, coming down.

"Have you both been out in this fog?" she scolded us. "Joan, I'm surprised at you. You should be more careful. You too, for that matter, Daisy. Maine fogs are known to be treacherous."

I said, "But it was lovely when we started out."

"That's our climate. Joan knows that." She glanced at both of us. "Have you had your lunch yet? Mrs. Vinton made chow mein for the children, and there's quite a bit left. Do you like chow mein? Will you have some?"

I love chow mein. I said yes without thinking. But when I caught Joan's expression, she seemed put out, as if she would not have accepted Frances' invitation as eagerly. It hadn't occurred to me that she did not want to be with Frances, but then I had scarcely scratched the surface of the Freers.

Frances led the way into her house-within-a-house. Unlike Joan's, it differed little from the atmosphere and tone of the big house. It was dim, shrouded with heavy drapes, and crowded with massive, carved pieces of furniture. I could imagine Frances preferring this style to Joan's, I could not see Frances fitting into Joan's dollhouse, but there was another reason. Joan told me while Frances was in the kitchen.

"Waste not, want not," said Joan, making a wry face. "Frances saw no reason to spend the money for a decorator and all that flimsy furniture they make these days, as she puts it. Frances is very like her mother. My father-in-law always admired Mother's thriftiness, and Frances tries to be exactly as she was. When these apartments were built, Frances went through the house and took whatever furniture could be spared from the other rooms."

Still, though the leather chairs were worn and the tables

too massive, there were handsome old Chinese porcelains about, and the polished floors glowed with antique Chinese rugs. I wondered if there had been Freers here in the days of the clipper ships and the China trade.

Frances returned with three glasses of sherry. "This will warm you up," she said, throwing herself so heavily into a chair that springs jingled.

Mrs. Vinton brought the tray with chow mein and added wood to the fire. I was hungry, the fire glowed, the wine warmed; this was one way to combat the gray gloom outside. Even Joan seemed more relaxed, and the talk was inconsequential, about styles. It was Joan who brought up the matter of my coat.

"With all those coats of Julia's hanging upstairs, I told Daisy it seemed foolish for her to buy one. You did put away several coats, didn't you, Frances?"

"I did, a scandalous lot of them," she said. "Did you ever hear of a woman buying clothes just to buy them, hardly wearing half of them? Personally I think it was an excuse to get herself off to New York. Ernest gave her a free hand, fool that he was over her."

"She enjoyed shopping, and Ernest didn't mind if it gave her pleasure," Joan said. "He could afford it."

"Ernest didn't mind?" Frances caught her up. "He did mind, very much. He wanted her here with him. But he gave in to her because he was afraid to lose her. And he lost her anyway." She looked satisfied.

I turned my head away. Her satisfaction was unpleasant.

Her glance was on me, appraising me. "Do you know, you're about the same height and build as Julia. I'm sure her things would fit you."

"I have all the clothes I need," I said. "Except for a coat. Besides, what I'll be needing soon are maternity clothes."

"Julia has those, too!" Frances's laugh was scornful. "Ernest went wild with joy when he found out she was pregnant. They went to New York together and bought out the town. It would just be a matter of hem lengths, but you could fix that."

She seemed totally disinterested in clothes, herself, or I would imagine her making use of Julia's. Her plaid slacks bagged in the seat, and her cardigan had had too many washings. But strangely, as with those worn, lustrous rugs beneath our feet, her hands were beringed with massive diamonds in old settings.

Amy brought in Moira and left her to play on the floor. I found myself following the baby's movements, and so did Joan. Were Joan's thoughts like mine? What will *my* baby be like?

Frances reached for Moira and cuddled her on her lap. She seemed self-conscious about this show of tenderness, and said almost with embarrassment, "Moira is especially precious, I suppose because she's the last."

"Three is a nice family," said Joan wistfully.

I said, "Why the last?"

"They had to remove the baby-making apparatus with Moira," Frances said bluntly.

But in spite of her matter-of-factness, her voice trembled. Frances minded, minded deeply.

"You could always adopt more children," I said.

The room fell into sudden silence. In surprise I looked at Frances and then at Joan, but their faces were blank. This was a delicate topic, why, I couldn't imagine.

Frances changed the subject.

"Have you had enough? There's more tea." When we both shook our heads, she rose and said, "Why don't we go up to the storage rooms so Daisy can pick herself out a coat?"

She carried Moira into the nursery, where Amy was with the other children, and then the three of us went up to the third floor, used for servants' rooms and storage. The house seemed to stretch endlessly, but everything was meticulously kept. Whatever one could say about Frances, she was a flawless housekeeper. The servants answered to her, and she was able to command this degree of perfection. As she led us through a series of storerooms, I had to express admiration for the way in which things were stored systematically, ticketed, packed in cartons, or hung in plastic.

"You're fantastic, Frances."

She flushed. "My father always said my mother could give lessons in how to run a perfect house. I wanted to keep it as he liked it."

She had finally found the closet she was looking for. "Here we are," she said, sounding like a saleslady in a store pulling out a rack in my size. And it did seem as if there were enough clothes hanging there to stock an elegant boutique. Even through the plastic bags I could see the magnificent sheen of fabrics, the glitter of sequins, the swelling of furs.

"Here's a coat," she said, untying the string at the neck of the bag, revealing a pale wool with a swoop of fox at the neck.

I shook my head, laughing. Not for taking walks on the cliff.

Frances uncovered a black coat, a silk raincoat, even a

mink coat. "It's a bit rubbed, it's the first Ernest bought her, and she wore it as if it were a rag, but it has years of wear left in it. Her new sable is here," she said, slapping at another bag.

"Why should she go away and leave a sable coat behind?" I said, awed at the extravagance of that gesture.

Frances said, "I've often wondered."

Her voice fell away. I stared from her to Joan in bewilderment. What was she implying. . . .

"Here's one," said Frances, and uncovered a heavy red tweed, with a long matching stole that could be useful to wrap about one's face in really cold weather. I put it on. It was very handsome, with a dramatic sweep of folds that could make it do for a long time. I certainly could not have afforded to buy one like it, not with one, two, or even three weeks' salary.

It was too much. "I can't take it," I mumbled.

"Don't be silly," said Frances brusquely. "Take it. The moths will get to it if you don't."

It was hard to imagine a moth finding its way through the cedar and the spray and the plastic.

Joan said, "Take it, Daisy. You look beautiful in it. You can always buy yourself a ski jacket for rough wear."

I took it, I carried it with me downstairs, and some of the delicious perfume the coat still carried seemed to have transferred to me. The presence of Julia had come disconcertingly close. I could smell her scent, I could almost see her, tall, with her high Portuguese coloring, striding in the folds of her red coat, the eyes of her husband following her.

We separated on the landing between the apartments, Frances to go in and take tea with her father in his room,

Joan and I to go back to our house. Already it had become mine, in less than a day, my home.

I hung the coat in my closet and joined Joan in our living room.

"Do you play Scrabble?" I said, determined to have no more gloomy talk.

"If you want."

I set up the board on the inlaid card table under the window. She sat opposite me, and we desultorily laid out a few words. My mind wandered first.

"Why did Frances react so strongly to adopting a child?"

"Did you notice?" she said. "I wondered if you had."

"It seemed rather odd today, with its being so common—"

"It was nothing to do with that," she said. "It's the will, you see. Or the trust fund, really. It was Frances who arranged about the trust; she got Father to withdraw a large block of stock from the company and convert it into a trust. The trust is to be shared equally by the natural children."

"*Natural* children?"

"It's run like a pool, and all the children will inherit when they are twenty-one. Until then the income from it goes to the parents. Frances and Walter, for instance, have that extra income. Ernest's went back into the pool when Ronnie died."

"But *natural* children—You mean, adopted children would not share?"

"That's the point," she said. "You see, Ernest and Julia only had Ronnie, and Julia swore she would rather die than have another. And as for us, I'd had two miscarriages, and there's always the chance I might never carry a child all the way. But Frances had three, and she didn't know at the time the trust was set up that Moira would be her last."

She said patiently, "Don't you see? If we adopted a child, or several, the income of the trust could be manipulated, the more children you had, the more income. That's why she put in that clause. She could safeguard the income for herself!"

I was stunned. Could Frances be that scheming? It scarcely seemed possible. I said, "It's hard to understand. Frances seems so incapable of such devious plotting—"

"You don't know Frances," she said with a ghost of a smile.

"But your father-in-law. How could he have allowed it?"

"My father-in-law," she repeated. "Who knows what he thinks or even how much he understands. We suspect his mind is clear sometimes and then clouds over, although Frances always insists he knows exactly what's going on. She has to maintain this, since she doesn't want any questions raised about the will."

"Do you think Mr. Freer knows nothing about it, then?"

"Oh, I suppose he approves of the general idea. Frances took advantage of Father's love for the children. It wasn't always this way. Once there was nothing as important to Father as the business, and Father grew to depend more and more on Amos, who was devoted to it and knew more about it than anyone except himself. Father knew that. If he'd been entirely clear-minded, he would have known that a freezer plant was essential right now and more important than the trust. After all, the children would inherit the business one day, they would be taken care of, but the new freezer plant was essential if the Fisheries is to continue as it has."

"Why did Frances do it?" I said. "I don't understand. She

must depend on the future of the business as the rest of you do."

"She couldn't stand it when Amos took over control. She always envied Ernest and Amos. When they were young, Father would take the boys to work at the plant during the summers when they were all home from school, but Frances had to stay home with her mother. Father believed the business was a rough place for a girl, and nothing Frances said or did could get him to change his mind. This was Frances' way of getting even. Of getting her hands on the profits."

"But why did your father-in-law allow it?" I said again.

"How much did he know, at the time?" she cried. "And anyway he began to change even before the first stroke; he began to change when my mother-in-law died. He began to lean on Frances. And Frances tried to take her mother's place. It was another way of getting control, you see."

"Why didn't Amos or Ernest persuade their Father to reconsider?"

"Ernest never cared that much one way or the other. He takes care of the fishing fleet, and the only things that mattered to him were Julia and Ronnie. Amos was the only one hurt, but he knew if he brought it up to Father, Father would think it was because we had no children and wouldn't benefit from the trust."

"Why should he even think that of Amos?" I cried, shocked.

"Because Frances has his ear, all the time, and that's what she would tell him. She has capitalized on the fact that when Father got sick and had to withdraw from the business, the only thing that interested him were the children. The children became all-important. That's why we're all here!"

she cried. "He drew up the will so that we would be forced to be near him, so he could be with the children all the time!"

She met my eyes, her own face white with sudden passion.

"What kind of will would insist we all live under one roof? Is it the thinking of a clear mind? It couldn't have been clear anymore! And Frances used him, took advantage of him! Who knows," she said, her voice falling, "she might even have hoped Julia would leave and Ernest would follow her to keep her and forfeit his share of the inheritance. And there would be more for her."

"Oh, *no*, Joan. I can't believe that."

"Can't you?" she said. "Well, maybe I might not have, once. She seems so pleasant and . . . ordinary on the surface. I know now that so many ordinary, pleasant people are like apples that seem smooth and sound when you look at them, but underneath there's that tiny worm that burrows through and through and destroys them."

Her words chilled me. The room had grown dusky as we talked, and I could scarcely make out the small edifice of words we had built on the Scrabble board. They all had so much of wealth. Could they have allowed the family to be ruptured by the desire for even more? Could it all be Joan's neurotic imaginings? I said, "Have you told any of this to Amos?"

"I learned most of it from Amos," she said quietly.

With a sudden gesture she scattered the words on the board, and then she looked up at me, and her face was again the pretty, eager face that she had lifted for Amos' kiss last night in the dining room.

She said, "Do you realize, Daisy, that I don't know a

single thing about you? Tell me what you're like; tell me what you did before you came here. Tell me about how you grew up and met . . . your husband. Everything!"

And so we talked until Amos came home. She really seemed to want to know about me, and her glance was warm and interested as I talked, and I could imagine what a different girl she might have been in a different setting, under different conditions. When she heard Amos' feet on the stairs, she jumped up at once and lit the lamps, transforming the room into the bright, flowering retreat she had made it, and opened the door for him.

They embraced, as hungry for each other as if they had just fallen in love. It was almost as if each had not believed that the other would really be there, and they clung now, gratefully.

I left them quietly. When I shut the door of my bedroom behind me, I had one of those moments when I felt very alone.

3

After that first week of learning to find my way about the house, of discovering the style of living that each family followed, of discovering Joan and Amos' particular pattern and how I was supposed to fit into it, the days began to go fast. Routine seems to be the best way to speed time along. I would catch myself often and wish that time would slow down. The future was bleak and uncertain. At least now my child was with me, and I was happy. I was under no strain, my problems taken care of for me. It was a kind of hiatus, and I did not want it to end too soon.

I gave Joan all my attention when she was alone, but as soon as Amos returned, I tried to leave them so they could spend their time together, in privacy. It was hard to have privacy in the confines of their small apartment, and the details of their lives were revealed too plainly. I knew the meaning of certain glances, of certain shades in their voices, of the closing of their door. I sometimes heard them late at night in their tiny kitchen, the murmurs, the hushed laugh, and I would think of them lying companionably close in their bed as Jed and I had done in the beginning when we still found delight in each other. I would think: How different it might have been if we could have yearned for this child as Joan and Amos yearned for theirs, how exciting to wait for its birth with a man you loved, who loved you.

But I had no regret for leaving Jed. The more intimately I shared Joan and Amos' life, the more I knew what a poor excuse for a marriage we had had. I thought of the times when I had offered Jed love and he had turned his back on me, irritated for a dozen irrelevant reasons, tired, bored, our quarters too hot, too cold, too sordid, too cramped, whatever, for reasons that would not have mattered if he had loved me.

When we spoke of my marriage, she was shocked.

"Couldn't you tell at once what kind of man he was?"

"I wanted to love him. I wanted it to work out. You don't know what it's like to be utterly alone. Even if your family is in California, you know you can reach them, you only have to pick up the telephone. Suddenly, with Jed, I belonged to someone. I wanted desperately for us to make a go of it."

"It's so unfair for you to bear this baby alone. It's so unfair to know you're going to give it up. I couldn't be as brave as you, ever."

"It isn't bravery. I have no choice."

She put her hand on mine. "I'm glad at least you have us. It makes me feel less useless." She smiled at her own words. "I have something to give you in return for your being here, even if it's only friendship."

"Only friendship!" I echoed. "You couldn't give me anything as important now!"

The weather grew colder, and the first snow of the season fell and quickly melted. The children still played outside, their voices ringing bright and sharp in the cold air. The playhouse shone like an icehouse, glittering with frost before the sun warmed up enough to melt it. Unless it rained, Sam continued to wheel Mr. Freer to his sheltered terrace, swathed in a fur rug, fur hat, and earmuffs, half his face frozen into the grimace that was the mark of his stroke, the other half smiling at the cries of the children. It was easy to understand Joan's feeling about him; it did seem as if he had stationed himself on the terrace to guard the children. Had he actually seen Ronnie drown? It was too dreadful to contemplate.

When Amos was home on weekends, I had to devise ways of keeping busy. Amy took every other Sunday off and went home with Sandy to her father's house in Bright River, and I often volunteered to stay with the children. Frances was delighted; she and Walter were free to drive off to visit friends or to stop at the sales still held in someone's barn where she could thriftily search out a good piece of old furniture, or a platter, or a fine old English spoon.

I enjoyed being with the children. Moira was docile and good-tempered, another Maggie, although Maggie had to be watched every minute or she would sturdily wander off by herself in pursuit of some secret quest. Jeffrey was different; Jeffrey stayed close. He would sidle up to me with an armful of books. "Read to me, Daisy?" he would ask shyly, his eyes like a fawn's. With the children, I forgot the tensions of the house, even why Amos had brought me here.

I sometimes wondered if Amos was satisfied with me. Although Joan no longer wanted me out of her sight, I could not see how I was helping her much. She seemed interested, even concerned about me, asking me often how I felt about the baby, about myself, about Jed, even about my childhood in Springfield, and yet in the middle of our conversation she would often lapse into a brooding silence that would worry me.

I mentioned it to Amos one night. Joan was in the bathroom doing her hair. She had canceled her appointment in Bright River because she had been too tense to subject herself to the hands of a hairdresser. I said soberly, "Am I doing her any good?"

"You're doing all that can be done," Amos said. "You don't know what she was before you came. She hasn't had a single crying spell since. She told me if you'd been her sister, she couldn't feel any closer."

I couldn't speak for a moment. But I felt the same for her, as if she were a frail younger sister, even though she was several years older.

"I'll talk to her doctor anyway, next time we see him," he said. "By the way, have you been to Raab yet?"

"Not yet. But I will make an appointment. I feel so well it hardly seems necessary."

He said, "I wish Joan could feel some of your confidence."

"You've rid me of most of my problems."

His eyes rested on me in a way I remembered from the first time we met, probing, and yet a part of him faraway and unseeing. We had spent little time together alone in the last few weeks, which was just as well. I was far too susceptible to Amos Freer, and I did not want to be. Most of the time when I saw him he seemed preoccupied, and Joan told me he was very much involved with the state of their business. But now, his glance studying me intently, he said, "Do you ever think about . . . your husband?"

"Sometimes," I admitted. "Not often. And when I do, it's to be glad it's over."

His eyes remained on me, thoughtfully. "What plans are you making, for afterward?"

I had that part all worked out. "There'll be enough money now, together with my student loan, to see me through my last year. And once I graduate, I'll get a job during the day and take my master's at night."

"And the baby?"

I said steadily, "I have no choice. I'll have to give it up for adoption. I've planned it that way from the beginning."

"Wouldn't it have been simpler," he said, "to have had an abortion at once? Giving up a child must be a painful experience."

"It would have been simpler, yes, but I couldn't do it." I explained how I felt. "I'm glad women can do it, who want it that way. I just didn't . . . want to."

my face and hair. It was a poor excuse for a path, and walking was difficult, but I felt fresh and happy enough not to notice. Every now and then it ended entirely and I was in a thicket of bushes, but it would open up suddenly on a new inlet, and the ocean beside me.

There were no houses at all except an occasional lean-to which looked as if it had been used by workmen, and the NO HUNTING PRIVATE PROPERTY signs nailed to the trees told me I was still on Freer land. It was like a small empire, and I thought: How proud one must feel to show it to one's child, and say, this is yours! Even if I could have kept my baby, what could I confer on him except my love? Instead of being surrounded by an adoring family who could lavish the world on him, he would even be separated from me while I worked, tended by indifferent hands.

But no. He would be adopted, and the agency would see to it that he was taken by a family who would cherish him and give him what he needed even if it was not a domain. I tried to put him out of my thoughts as I did most of the time. He was still little enough of an encumbrance, though more and more I was aware of his presence inside me.

I squared my shoulders and bit into the apple I had brought with me. I thought of Amos, and how different it would be for the baby if he'd had a father like Amos, and I was not even thinking now of the family traditions, of the wealth. It wasn't easy to live close to a man like Amos. I had known a year and a half of married life, the early part of it passionate, and being so near Amos and Joan provoked too many memories. We had begun to grow so at ease with one another as to be careless. Amos would come into the dining room on weekend mornings in robe and slippers, and even his early-morning look stimulated memories, the rough shadow of his beard, the hair at the neck of his pajamas, the unexpected slenderness of his feet and ankles. It would have been very easy to fall in love with him even if I didn't like him as much. If I didn't care for Joan as much.

I had hardly noticed the fog moving in. At first it was gauzy as chiffon, obscuring, clearing again, and I took it for the onset of evening. I looked at my watch, and saw it was only half past three.

Time to turn back. In fact, I had walked too far. If it had taken me two hours to come this far, it would be dark before I returned home. I quickened my pace.

The fog deepened. At water level the thrust of the waves was so loud I could hear them even when I could no longer see them. Inland it was even worse, a dense gray world. Now and then I would blunder into a branch and snap it with a startling crack, or a hidden twig would scratch my cheek. The trouble was, I was growing tired, and trying to walk faster was making me more tired still. I thought of Dr. Raab's prescription of light exercise: Would four hours of walking come under that category?

The path climbed now, so I knew at least I was approaching the cliffs. I stopped to catch my breath. I'd been foolish. Would Joan and Amos have begun to worry? I pushed on, more slowly. It was dark when I felt myself on the frozen earth of the cliff walk.

I would be home in half an hour. I allowed myself the luxury of sitting down on a rock. I was damp with exertion, damp with spray, and when I sat down, the cold crept into me, chilling me to the bone.

I rose stiffly, feeling even more like a fool. Every step was an effort, and at best I could only see a few feet in front of me. I gasped with relief when at last some distance beyond I glimpsed the faint pearly glow of floodlights. They had turned them on; they missed me. They might even be looking for me. I walked as fast as I could, my eyes straining to see the path in the furry darkness. Could I have harmed the baby? My back was beginning to hurt, and it had never hurt before—

A large shape loomed in front of me, blocking the path.

My knees turned to water. Maybe it was a bush—No, it was moving, quietly, toward me.

In panic I took a step backward and fell. The ocean dropped down sheer on one side; there was nothing under part of me. I inched back, reaching out for the slatted snow fence that moved as I grasped it.

A man stood above me; his hands seized my arms.

I screamed. And screamed.

I was pulled to my feet.

"You," said the voice. Ernest's voice.

"Don't touch me!"

He let go. We were close enough to see each other's faces now. His eyes were staring in his white face.

"It's her coat," he said thickly. "Her perfume."

Now I could understand. He was as shocked as I was. He had thought me Julia.

"Get back to the house," he said in that thick, shaken voice. "They're looking for you."

I stumbled forward again in the direction of the floodlights. I could hear him walking behind me. We crossed the truck garden. We reached the smoothness of the lawn. In the comparative brightness of the floodlights I turned.

"Frances gave me the coat. It was hanging in the store-room. I didn't think it would matter if—"

"The bitch," he said. "She had no right to touch her things."

"Here!" I cried. "You can have it back!" I started to struggle out of the sleeves, but he stopped me. Again I felt the grip of hard hands, forcing the coat closed over me.

"You fool! I don't want the damned coat!"

We stared at each other.

"I'm sorry," he muttered. "I could even smell her perfume. You walk like her. In the fog . . . I'm sorry."

He strode abruptly toward the house.

I followed, trembling.

When I let myself into the hall, I was surrounded at once, by Joan, by Frances and the children. Walter and Amos had each taken a car and gone to look for me. They did not imagine I was so foolhardy as to walk in this fog beside the ocean. Only Ernest—Had Ernest found me? they asked.

By the time Amos came back I was warmed by hot soup and tea. He was angry with me. I had really frightened him.

"Don't ever do anything as reckless as that again, Daisy!"

When I lay in my bed that night, I went over what had happened, quailing with shame. Why had I been so terror-stricken? It wasn't like me to succumb to pointless terror, and yet it was terror that I felt there on the cliffs. It could have been a madman; I could have been pushed off. Anyone could have been pushed off and never found again, washed out to sea or recovered only when no longer recognizable. But who would do it? Only a madman.

Nonsense, I told myself sternly. You behaved like an idiot there on the path, screaming your head off.

I thought of Ernest's face, white with shock. As if he had seen a ghost, the ghost of Julia.

Where was Julia? Why had she vanished so suddenly, leaving those beautiful clothes, the sable coat, behind? Not a note, not a word. Why did Ernest stalk the cliff walk?

It would be easy to push someone from those cliffs into the turbulent sea. Julia?

4

How to explain the change that came over me after that night? Reality to me has always been a sunny place. I don't know why, precisely; it isn't as if I am insensitive to the ugliness and despair of existence. I've known death: My father died when I was old enough to need him and miss him; my mother died and shattered the fabric of my world. I've known misery and failure, with Jed, and poverty, too. And yet deep within me is an unquenchable essence which has always responded joyously to life. Maybe this was the only reason why I could not allow a doctor to insert an instrument into that microscopic blob of tissue in my womb or drown it in a salt solution.

Up to that moment on the fog-wreathed cliff when I was so sure I was facing at best an assault by a madman, if not death, the problems of the Freers were beyond me, problems I could view objectively and explain rationally. But no more. Now it was as if I had fallen under the same evil spell, as if I shared the family's danger and its fate.

It did no good to tell myself I was foolish, that it had grown out of a mistake, that it was Julia's walk and Julia's coat and Julia's perfume that Ernest had attacked on the path, not me. And had he attacked me? Might he not have tried to hold me back from falling? But the expression on his face—

Fear is insidious. Reason doesn't explain its beginnings, its inroads; logic can't dispel it; common sense can't laugh it away. I felt a cold breath of danger around me.

I had to fight it, if only for Joan's sake. If I ever allowed myself to succumb to it, I would be no good at all to her. I reminded myself that it was only Ernest of the whole household who had threatened me, and he was just recovering from a nervous breakdown. But Ernest had been hostile to me from the start; I had sensed his response that first night I came to their table, and so it must be something else other than the shock I had given him on the cliffs. Had he seen a resemblance to her in me that night at the table? Or was it only that a disturbed man would regard all strangers with suspicion?

And if he thought me Julia on the cliff, why the violence of his reaction? What had happened between him and Julia before she left?

Whenever I could, I tried to bring the conversations between Joan and me around to Julia, but Joan could offer nothing. Frances was more revealing. Frances, I think, regarded me as something of an innocent, or at best a younger sister, someone with whom she could be open and free without fear of consequence. She began to look for opportunities to talk to me: I was a repository for thoughts she had bottled up inside her. Like her jealous love of her father.

She once told me that though her father had never cared for Julia, once he learned she was to have a child, he had asked Frances to allow Julia to sit beside him at table.

"It wasn't as if I hadn't two children of my own at the time," she said, the wound still fresh in her voice.

I didn't dare ask her why it had mattered so much.

She said, with satisfaction, "Of course, that all changed once I was pregnant with Moira."

I wondered if her jealousy would extend to Joan, now that her baby would be born, knowing she could no longer compete, but Frances was careful to say nothing derogatory about Joan to me. She did add, however, "Haven't you noticed how Father dotes on Joan? He never did, before."

I brought the talk back to Julia. "You said Mr. Freer never cared for Julia. Why?"

"Father had heard the same stories we all did about her," she said. "Ernest was just twenty-two when he married her. He didn't have to. But he was young and inexperienced. There were plenty of men in Bright River who didn't marry her. We knew it would turn out badly, and it did. When my brother woke up to the kind of woman she was, they fought like cats and dogs. We could hear them in the apartment below ours. I remember once"—she hesitated, but couldn't resist going on—"once Walter happened to mention that he'd seen Julia in Bright River having a drink with an old boyfriend of hers at the local pub where all the fishermen hang out. He only told me, but I thought Ernest should know, and I told him."

I was shocked. Her color heightened.

"I did think he should know. Everyone in town knew. But all he did was tell me to mind my own business." Blood still mottled her cheeks. "Why should she make a fool of him? Who was she, to treat Ernest the way she did?"

But I did not think her anger was out of love for Ernest. Her eyes raked me, to see if she had gone too far.

"Not that Julia got off unscathed, mind you. Ernest is slow to explode, but when he does, the pieces fly. I am sure there were times when he struck her. I once saw a bruise on her cheek—But of course, she wouldn't mind. These people expect that kind of treatment from their husbands."

I could imagine Ernest furious enough to strike her. Amos could never be roused to such a fury, Amos would only retreat into himself. I remembered Ernest's voice that night when he'd called Frances a bitch, I remembered the fury in his hands when he had pulled the coat back around me.

"Why didn't Julia ask for a divorce?"

"I suppose she knew she couldn't win in any divorce action. She had made her name a scandal in Bright River."

"Did she have money? How does she live now?"

"How do we know? There hasn't been a word from her. Still, knowing Julia, I'd be willing to gamble she's found someone to pick up the tab for her."

I marveled at the spite in her voice even now. It would have been impossible to disguise how she felt from Ernest or Julia even if she'd known some subtlety, and Frances did not.

Joan's response to Julia was unmistakably her own.

"I couldn't understand how she could have had such a darling child and yet neglect her so. She was always going somewhere on some pretext or other, Acapulco, New York, the Caribbean, leaving Ronnie to Amy and their maid. She went alone most of the time, because Ernest couldn't get away. It was terrible for Ernest."

"Why did he let her go?"

"Why? How could he stop her? He loved her, and he would have done anything, I suppose, if he had thought it would save their marriage."

I said, "Lucky for Ronnie she had other children to play with. She wouldn't miss her mother that much."

Joan didn't answer at first. Then she blurted out, "Frances didn't bother to hide her dislike of Ronnie."

"But why? Ronnie was a child!"

"Frances is jealous of anyone that Father shows an interest in. Ronnie was a wild, pretty little thing, like Julia. She would climb all over Father, sit in his lap, hug him, and kiss him. Of course Father adored her and showed it plainly. Frances' children are like Frances. You know, rather stolid and not particularly affectionate. So Frances resented Ronnie."

"Was Ernest aware of it?"

"How could he help but be? And Julia knew it, too. Women are quicker about these things, and I'm sure they must have talked about it. When Ronnie died, there was a terrible scene. Ernest said to Frances, 'Don't try and pretend you're sorry!'"

I caught my breath.

"Ernest blames Frances for other things. For making Freer's Cove so unpleasant that Julia didn't want to stay here. Maybe it might all have turned out differently if—" She lifted her shoulders.

I was speechless for a few moments, marveling at the antagonisms that could grow up between members of a family. But then I am an only child, and I had always envied households with many children in them.

"Her own brother," I said slowly. "It seems to me if I had

a brother, I would only want him to be happy. If he wanted Julia, that would be enough."

Her lips tightened; her nostrils turned white with sudden feeling. "You don't know the Freers," she said intensely. "You don't know what they're capable of."

I cried, "Not all of them, Joan. Not Amos."

"No, of course. Not Amos." Her voice softened; the anger went out of it. She looked at the clock. It was almost time for him to come home.

III

✻

✻

✻

1

IT WAS THANKSGIVING.

Joan and Amos were leaving that weekend for New York, for a checkup with Joan's doctor. They had invited me to come with them, but I knew I was not needed when she was away from Freer's Cove; she would be completely happy alone with Amos. I told them thanks, but that I'd enjoy a lazy few days at home.

What I did not say was that I was still unsure of my emotions, revisiting New York. It was true that Jed had lost any hold he might have had since the day I left him, but how would I feel if I were again in the city where we were once, briefly, happy? Curiosity might push me to find out if he'd had a change of heart since my absence. Had he tried to find me? Was he interested in how I was? These were precisely the reactions Amos had warned me about. It was better not to expose myself to them. I have always acted on impulse; I might even act foolishly, out of pity.

They were leaving after dinner. Frances had determined

that Thanksgiving was one of the occasions when her father would like to see all his children and grandchildren together. If they had to leave too late to reach New York by night, Amos said, they would stop somewhere on the way and continue in the morning.

There was more lightheartedness than usual around the table that day. Except for Moira, the children were present, which made it noisier, and then Walter had mixed martinis for all of us instead of our usual predinner sherries. Even Amos had more than one, so that dinner was delayed, but none of us minded because the hour was so cheerful. Ernest was not present, which may have helped. He turned up only as we were sitting down to table, to Frances' annoyance. She seemed to feel he had deliberately flouted the festivities to spite her.

But the good humor persisted during dinner, buoyed by several bottles of wine. By the time we moved to the library for brandy and Madeira Amos had even managed to draw Ernest into the conversation. They reminisced about how they had carried on when they were Sandy and Jeff's age, how they used to sneak out after being put to bed to go ice skating on the pond at the far side of the property.

"Remember when I fell in and you pulled me out, Ernest?"

"I knew what I would have caught if I hadn't," Ernest said, and even grinned.

Jeffrey and Sandy listened, openmouthed. I suppose it was especially hard for them to imagine these reserved adults acting up and being disobedient. Sandy was with us at dinner because he had been invited to spend the night in Jeff's room while Walter and Frances were in Portland visiting friends.

Jeffrey's thin fluting voice cried, "Didn't they look in your bed and see you weren't there?"

"We rolled up blankets and stuck them under the quilts, to look like us," Amos said. "The only time we were caught was when your mother asked to go along and we wouldn't let her, and she squealed on us to your grandpa."

Mr. Freer made a sound like a laugh, so he may have been following our conversation, or maybe he only laughed because we were.

"Male chauvinism," grumbled Frances. "I skated as well as either of you."

"Uncle Ernest," said Jeffrey, "when is the pond going to be hard enough for skating?"

"I think it's hard enough now," Ernest said. "I was out on it last night."

"Hey, then we can go right now!" Sandy cried. "How about it, Jeff?"

"Now just a moment," Frances said. "You can't go out there alone, and Amy can't go with you because Mrs. Vinton is gone for the day and she has to be with Moira and Maggie."

Sandy looked disgusted; Jeff stole a look at his face and went up to Frances.

"Ah, Mom! Please?"

The sun was already low, the light glancing orange into the library, brightening the dark bindings of the books.

"Daddy and I have to leave soon or we'd go with you," Frances said uncertainly.

Ernest said awkwardly, "I'll take them to the pond."

There was a palpable silence, and then a swift look between Frances and Walter. Almost at once, smoothly, Walter said, "I suppose I might go, too, for about an hour. Do me good. Work off some of that dinner."

"Your martinis were blockbusters," Amos said.

"You didn't turn down that second one, I noticed."

"But I'd better have a nap before I try driving to New York. Coming, Joan?"

It was one of the few times I was sorry to see a family gathering break up. I followed Joan and Amos to their apartment, thinking I might nap, too, my head felt so heavy, but then I changed my mind and decided what would be best for me would be some fresh air. I put on coat and mittens and walked down toward the pond.

It was more than a pond, a small lake actually, the far end of it almost out of sight behind clumps of birch and pine. I could hear the ring of the skates and the children's voices as I neared the bank. Sandy was managing expertly, bent over as he raced by. Walter had Jeffrey by the arm as Jeffrey took a few steps, teetered, and then tried again, his face absorbed with the determination to follow Sandy.

I watched so intently, rooting for Jeff silently when he managed to stay upright for longer and longer intervals, that I didn't notice Ernest some distance away, almost hidden by the trees. He too was watching the children, such a brooding expression on his face that I could only imagine his thoughts were of his daughter and how he might be guiding her now just as Walter guided Jeff. My heart was wrenched with sudden pity, and on impulse I went up to him. He started; he'd been too deep in his thoughts to observe me.

"Why don't you join them? If I weren't afraid of falling, I might, myself."

"I don't care to skate anymore," he said, briefly, barely

glancing at me out of sore, hostile eyes, and started back almost at once toward the house.

I stayed on, smarting from his rebuff, until it became too dark to see, and Walter finally rounded up the boys; we walked home together.

Amy was waiting for me when I reached our apartment.

"Daisy, Mrs. Freer said it was all right to ask you. I hate to bother you, it's being holiday and all, but I guess you won't be going anywhere tonight anyway, so—" She flushed. "See, I have a kind of important date tonight, and they never told me before I couldn't have the night off, and—"

"And you'd like me to see that the children get to bed. Of course, Amy. You go ahead with your plans. I don't mind at all."

I had put the children to bed before when Walter and Frances wanted to get away and Amy was off. Mrs. Vinton, like Minna and like Mr. Freer's cook, always left after dinner. I had little enough to do, and I enjoyed being with the children. "When do you want me to come over?"

"I can bathe Moira and get her in her crib. It's only Maggie that needs help with her bath. The boys will take their own showers, so they're no problem, if you can stand the racket they make when they sleep in the same room. I told Sandy already he better behave or he won't be invited again, but you know how boys are."

"Don't worry about them. Just knock on my door when you're ready to leave."

I liked Amy and felt sorry for her. She had been the girl who, in the language of Bright River, had got herself into trouble and disgraced her father. I could understand how anxious she was to marry again and have a real home for

Sandy, and I could imagine how important each date was to her, how full of expectancy she was that this might be the one, the lucky one.

Amos and Joan were still sleeping when I heard Amy's light tap on my door. I jumped up quickly to answer it before she should wake them. She looked handsomely turned out in a furred coat that might also have been one of Julia's, cut down: it looked too splendid for Amy to have afforded it any more than I could have afforded my red one.

"They'll be leaving any minute now," she said. "The baby is asleep, and I've warned the boys I'll have their hides if they wake her up. You can put Maggie to bed anytime. She's a good sleeper, that one."

"I'll come right over now. And you have a good time, Amy."

"Thanks. And remember, don't take any guff from Sandy."

She left the apartment door open for me. I could still hear Walter's voice from the bedroom, hurrying Frances along, and a commotion from the boys' room. I looked in. Sandy had been prancing around, followed by Jeff, whose eyes shone and whose cheeks burned; plainly, Sandy was his idol. I shut their door to muffle the noise and went in to fill the tub for Maggie.

Maggie was a solid lump of pink flesh, endearing in her constant good humor. Placidly she allowed me to soap and rinse and dry her. I couldn't help but think what a pity she and Jeff could not have exchanged characteristics, how he might have benefited from some of her sturdiness and solidity, while she might have used his gentleness and grace.

Walter and Frances looked in on Maggie before they left. Frances was wearing a faded mink coat, and her shoes were too ornate. "I left some cocoa on the stove for the boys. It might quiet them down."

"Suppose they won't drink it?"

"Close their door and let them tear the walls down, as long as they don't wake up Moira and Maggie."

Maggie picked out a large Dr. Seuss book for me to read. But her eyes drooped heavily before I was halfway through, and when I closed the book, she did not hear me turn out the lights and tiptoe out.

I met Amos in the corridor as I headed for the boys' room. He was carrying a cup of coffee for me in his hand.

"Joan made it fresh just now," he said, handing it to me. "Both of us had a tough time waking up after this afternoon, and we needed it to get going."

"It smells good." I sipped some. "I think the boys will keep me up even if I get sleepy." I noticed he already had his overcoat on, and a small valise stood by the door. "Are you leaving now? Is Joan ready?"

"Here she is."

Joan was emerging from her apartment. She looked delicate in her dark furs, with small diamonds dangling from her ears. I saw them in a new light, or rather, in a light I was not accustomed to seeing them, as a handsome, wealthy young pair off to weekend at a luxurious hotel, their proper milieu. We were so familiar and casual here that I had almost forgotten the difference between us, and they had made me feel their equal.

"You both look wonderful!"

But they didn't. They looked taut and strained. There were dark circles under Amos' eyes and a twitching near his mouth like a tic. He must be more apprehensive about this visit to her gynecologist that he had ever let on.

Joan kissed me. "I hope you won't be too lonely."

"With all those kids? Have a good trip, and lots of luck with the doctor!"

I went to the window facing the front of the house and watched their car circling the drive, and then I returned to the boys' room. I was surprised to see the lights out, the boys in their beds. I was not so naïve that the thought didn't occur to me that they were up to something, but I said only, "Have you had your showers?"

It was Jeffrey who piped up, "Do we have to, Daisy? We're very *clean*."

Sandy gave an elaborate yawn. "We're very sleepy, too."

I didn't believe them. Still, it was possible. They'd been skating in the cold; they'd been carrying on all the time I was putting Maggie to bed; they'd eaten more dinner than usual—it was possible that even a five- and a six-year-old might get sleepy after all of that. I was more heavy-eyed myself than I expected to be, in spite of my coffee.

"Would you like some cocoa?"

"Unh-unh."

"It'd help you to sleep."

"We don't need it. We're sleepy already."

"And shut the door, Daisy," called Jeff. "Mama lets me sleep with the door shut."

If it were some game, I'd find out soon enough. I went back to the living room and finished the last of my coffee. Gosh, I was sleepy! I tried to rouse myself by going into the kitchen and washing out the pot of cocoa Frances had left on the stove, and my coffee cup and saucer, too.

Maybe TV would help. But the boys would hear it from their room and it might wake them up again. I decided against it until I was sure they were asleep. All three bedrooms were silent. Amazing, I thought, blinking to keep my eyes open. I went to the casement windows and flung them open, thinking the cold air would revive me.

Frances' windows, too, looked out on the back lawn and the playground. I still had not overcome my first reaction to the look of the playground by night. There was a full moon turning it to silver-white, and the tall witch loomed above the maze, her phosphorescent eyes and jagged smile gleaming faintly. Perhaps it was only the small sad ghost of poor Ronnie that made it seem so ominous at night, without the children playing in it.

I thought of Ernest, as he had leaned against the trunk of a birch and watched the children. What was on his face: Was it bitterness, or even envy? Or just the anguish of memory? I felt cold touch me deep inside: to know the death of a child—

I must try to be more tolerant of his manner, I must try to understand the depth of his despondency and at least not let him upset me. Why should it matter to me, his curtness, his hostility? It was not Ernest I had to live with. And yet it was disturbing to feel that hostility directed against me without reason.

Even as I stared down, hypnotically, I saw him emerge through the patio doors and cut across the lawn. It was unmistakably Ernest, even to my sleepy eyes: I could recognize his long stride, his shoulders slightly hunched against the cold. He was heading toward the cliffs again, on his solitary nightly walk, as if he were fretting over that nighttime desolation of wind and water and rocks, as if he were drawn there inexorably, waiting, searching.

I shivered. I shut the window and turned back gratefully to the warmth of the room. I had not returned to the cliffs since that night. I was afraid of meeting him. I was *afraid;* there it was. I told myself I need not be, I told myself that Sam was in the house, and Mr. Freer, and at least one of the maids, and Cory was in the gatehouse; but they were old, or ill, or women, and Ernest was strong. I was ashamed of myself for doing it, but I went to the outer door of the apartment and locked it. I had barely reached the sofa before I succumbed to sleep: I couldn't fight it anymore.

It was Walter's key in the lock that waked me. I sat up, blinking at Walter and Frances, who were red-faced from the cold and still in their heavy coats.

"Poor Daisy, weren't we dreadful to keep you up so late!"

"What time is it?" I looked at my watch. It said almost three. "It doesn't matter, I've been sleeping most of the time."

"You mean the kids let you?" Walter's voice was thicker than usual. Plainly drinks had been served in Portland, too.

"Ssh, don't wake them now," said Frances, moving off to her room. "I can hardly keep my eyes open. Good night, Daisy! Sleep late tomorrow!"

As I left them, I heard her tell Walter, "It was the cocoa. Hot cocoa at bedtime does it every time."

It hardly seemed important to tell her that they hadn't been awake long enough to drink the cocoa. I did feel a little guilty for not having looked in on the children, but Frances and Walter had ducked off to bed before I had time hardly to mention it to them. I went through the long dimly lit hall to our own apartment and found I was glancing apprehensively over my shoulder. Once I let myself in, I went through each room before I went into mine. It isn't like me to be as nervous, and I made myself laugh at my actions. It isn't like me to have a headache, either, and yet my head felt heavy. Maybe it was from sleeping at an odd angle on the sofa. Even in my bed I continued to have an odd, uneasy feeling. I told myself what my mother used to tell me when I was a child: Things will look different in the morning.

But not that morning.

Someone was pounding on my head.

I sat up. Gray light filled the room. It was dawn. The pounding. . . .

The pounding came from outside. Someone was knocking repeatedly on my door. I staggered out of bed to open it. Frances stood there in her robe, her cheeks the color of putty. My first thought was, she's had too much to drink, and she isn't used to it; she has a hangover.

She said, "Where is Jeffrey?"

I could feel the blood drain from my face. My lips wouldn't move.

"Daisy, we can't find Jeffrey."

"I don't understand," I said stupidly.

"He's not in his bed."

"But he must be." I could hear my own voice ringing hollowly in what felt like a great empty cavern in my head.

"He isn't. Where could he be?"

I managed to collect my thoughts. "Sandy will know!" I cried. "They slept together."

"Sandy doesn't know. We asked him. He went back to sleep in Amy's room last night."

"But he couldn't have! I saw them in bed together. The lights were out and they were going to sleep. . . ."

The shock was clearing my head. I remembered that I had fallen asleep scarcely half an hour after I had left them. I had suspected their unexpected quiet, but I hadn't stayed awake long enough to check on them to see if they had stayed in their beds. I met Frances' eyes miserably.

"I don't know what came over me last night. I suppose I'm not used to drinking, the wine on top of the martini. . . . They were in bed and I assumed—"

"They heard Ernest and Amos talking," she said dully. "About how they would leave rolled-up blankets under the covers. We found the blankets there this morning." She turned away from me, biting her lip.

I felt sick with guilt. "How was he dressed?"

"His hooded coat is missing, and his mittens."

"Then maybe he went out early to play!"

"Walter is looking for him. He hasn't come back."

"I'll get dressed and help find him."

I dressed hurriedly, putting a cap over my hair and wearing boots. I could think only of the playground. Somewhere in that playground— I went down into the hall.

Amy met me, her face gaunt. "I've covered every inch of house," she said thinly. "There's no sign of him. I should never have left them."

"I'm to blame, not you. But don't talk this way. We'll find him. It's some game he's playing."

Sandy materialized from somewhere, pale and frightened.

Amy turned when she heard him. "You go help find him, hear me!" she said harshly.

I reached out and took his mittened hand in mine. "Let's look together, okay, Sandy?"

He didn't answer, only came along with me.

"Give me a hint, Sandy," I said casually, as we went out through the patio doors. "Didn't Jeff tell you something?" I was sure he had some knowledge of where Jeffrey was. He looked too frightened, and there were tearstains on his cheeks.

He shook his head. "Don't know."

"Show me the way into the maze."

I followed him, my heart beginning to thump heavily. I don't know what I expected to find, but at every new turn I felt a wrench of fear inside me. The playground seemed without life in the early-morning quiet. We were at the heart of it now, and no Jeffrey. I turned to him.

"Where else do you like to play, Sandy? Could he have gone to the cliffs?"

I did not think so. The children were not allowed there.

"The barns? The road to Bright River? The pond?"

His hand jerked free of mine, and he bolted off, leaving me alone. If ever I had seen terror on a child's face, this was it. It froze me, and for a moment I could only stare after where he had gone.

The pond.

The frantic, terrible surmise robbed me of what was left of my sense of direction. I don't know how long it took me to get out of the maze, stumbling against the frozen bare hedges, up against a dozen dead ends. At last I was free, and I almost ran past the outbuildings and onto the cleared ground that led down to the pond.

Walter was standing on the edge.

"Walter?" My voice was a breath.

He turned a ravaged face toward me.

"That's Jeff's hat, caught on the edge of the ice." He was pointing, and now I saw several neat round holes sawed through the surface of the pond that was marked only with the whorls and cuts of the children's skates. Walter had not touched the hat. The pompon was held by a jagged point of ice.

I did not dare ask him if he had looked any further. He said in a dull voice, "Ernest went to town for help. They'll have to break up the ice."

My legs would not hold me up. I leaned against a tree, trembling. And then I saw a pair of skates near the path that led down to the lake. A child's skates, flung down as if in haste, one some distance from the other.

Walter must have seen them. I had to be sure. "Walter, these skates—"

He turned. "They're Sandy's. I bought them for him myself. They were here, last night or early this morning, Jeff and Sandy."

"But those holes in the ice. They weren't here."

"Someone must have been fishing during the night. We know that people from around Bright River come here to fish. We never stop them. There's carp as well as eels in the pond. There's been nobody there till now, I guess because the ice wasn't hard enough, I don't know for sure why; only I know there weren't any holes yesterday when we were skating or we would have seen them, down at this end any-way."

His voice went on in an odd monotone, as if he were talking only to hold on to himself.

"The kids wouldn't have seen the holes at night, until they were right on them, even with the full moon. And by that time it'd be too late. Jeff's a bad skater. He's just learning. He would never have been able to stop in time."

He buried his face in his hands and began to sob. Help-lessly I watched him, crying myself, until he said chokingly, "Go to Frances. Stay with her."

I was glad to get away from the pond, but I did not want to have to tell Frances. She was waiting for me. When she saw my face she cried out.

"Where was he?"

"It's not sure, Frances. The pond—"

She brushed away my arms fiercely and ran outside. Somehow I found the presence of mind to call Sam away from Mr. Freer and tell him. We huddled together, staring at each other.

"Best to keep Mr. Freer out of it as long as we can."

Cars were coming up the driveway, a truck with metal equipment jolting on its open back. And then an ambu-lance.

"Best keep him to the other side of the house," said Sam.

I found Amy in the nursery with Maggie and the baby. Maggie kept asking for Jeff and Sandy, but we put her off. She would go back to her doll again, but her placidness was shattered, and after a while she would return to say fret-fully, "Where are they? When are they coming home?"

I knew how worried Amy must be about Sandy; each time Maggie asked about the boys it was an effort to answer her casually, and her mouth would pinch tight in the corners, making two deep folds in her cheeks. Now and then she would stare out of the window, but surreptitiously, as if she did not want even me to guess her fears.

It was several hours before I heard them come into the hall below. We stayed upstairs with the children until Walter brought Frances in and left her with us while he went out again.

I followed her into the living room.

She did not lift her head. "They found him. His skates were still on. How he managed to strap them on so well . . . but Sandy must have helped him."

She wept, her face mottled and distorted, and through my own grief I could feel the thrust of her anger directed against me. I couldn't blame her. I was too heartsick over Jeff to care about her anger or blame. But I felt horror, too. And fear.

I don't know when I first remembered about Amos and Joan. Someone would have to call them. They hadn't been sure at which hotel they would stay, and at the time it hadn't seemed important to know. I thought, thank God she wasn't here this morning. She would have to be told, but at the proper time, quietly. And yet, how to tell it properly, or quietly, news of a second child's death, a third child who might have died, what other way could she possibly react?

It was several hours before they came back, Walter and Ernest, and with Dr. Raab. Ernest seemed jolted out of his remoteness. His face looked stark and grim over his brown beard, and I thought: He is reliving the day when they found Ronnie. Mrs. Vinton brought hot coffee, and we all drank it gratefully.

Dr. Raab insisted he administer a sedative to Frances. She permitted him, her eyes red-rimmed and staring.

"When did the boys leave the house?" she asked thickly.

"We won't know for sure until we find Sandy. But if Sandy spent the night with his mother, and she says she found him in her room when she came home, then it must have been before midnight," Walter said. He took Frances' hands in his as if he needed her touch as much as she his. "What difference does it make, darling? What good does it do to know?"

My mouth was dry. "Why didn't I hear them leave?"

"How could you? You were asleep." The accusation was there.

I looked down. Behind me I heard Dr. Raab saying in a low voice to Ernest, "The tests will show how long he was in the water." It was more than I could bear. The image struck me like a blow in the stomach. I stood up hurriedly and barely reached the bathroom before I vomited. When I finally stopped and opened the door, Dr. Raab was waiting for me.

"I'm going to give you a sedative too, Daisy," he said, and took me firmly by the arm and led me back to my room.

"Frances hates the sight of me," I said in my despair. "I don't know how I could have gone to sleep, it isn't like me at all to be sleepy so early, and I don't know what came over me, but then she did tell me to shut the boys' door and leave them—"

He was rolling up my sweater sleeve. I was too distraught to feel the needle.

"I don't blame her for blaming me—"

"Daisy," he said quietly, "you wouldn't expect Frances to behave rationally today, would you? You just ignore what she says for a while. And be kind. She'll need that. And after a while I know she'll be more clearheaded about what happened."

The injection worked swiftly, and I could hear my voice going on incessantly, incoherently. Dr. Raab was easing me onto my unmade bed, pulling off my shoes, covering me.

"Ernest hates me, too. I don't know why. I've hardly even spoken to him. Why doesn't he trust me? I can feel he doesn't trust me—"

My voice was running down at last, like a bad phonograph record, fainter, no more words to say. . . .

Dr. Raab sat on the edge of my bed, patting my hand, and to my blurred eyes his long furrowed state of Maine face topped with a square cut of graying hair looked beautiful; he was my friend, my only friend here—

"The Freers are a queer lot," said his voice soothingly. "They're tough and hard and tenacious, once they get their teeth into anything, but there's a weakness. Maybe it's come down through the mother. Mrs. Freer never spoke another word after her daughter Ann died. Weak strain somewhere . . . low tolerance to emotional pressure . . . likely. . . ."

I fell asleep with my hand in his. When I awoke, I was alone. It took me some minutes to remember why I was in bed fully dressed with the sun still high outside. Memory returned bit by dreadful bit. I got up and smoothed my hair. But there was no running away from it. I made myself return to Frances' apartment.

2

The apartment was quiet and seemed deserted, but I found Mrs. Vinton in the kitchen. When she offered me a sandwich, I became aware for the first time that I'd had nothing but coffee all day. But for once my infallible appetite had deserted me: I shook my head.

"Where is everybody?"

"Mrs. Freer's sleeping. Doctor must have given her something real strong."

"And the children?"

"Poor things. Only the two of them left now," she said, shaking her head as if they too were doomed. "Heaven help them. Amy took them out. Maggie was getting fidgety."

"Sandy isn't back?"

She shook her head again. "Amy's half out of her mind. But she won't show it. Her boy knows something."

"Are they looking for Sandy?"

"Mr. Walter and Mr. Ernest both took cars."

We were silent. "Someone should get in touch with Amos."

"They located them," she said. "They're on their way home now."

I pictured their drive home and their state of mind, and my spirits sank even deeper. I left her and went downstairs just as the front door opened and Amy and the children came in.

"They found Sandy. Mr. Ernest has him in the car," she said hurriedly, pushing Maggie toward the stairs. "I have to get the kids settled in the nursery so I can speak to him."

"Let me take the children," I said.

It almost seemed to me she hesitated, but then maybe I was too sensitive to the part I had played in the tragedy. "Would you, Daisy? Thanks."

I carried Moira upstairs into the nursery, while Maggie tagged behind. Mrs. Vinton joined me, and together we pulled off overshoes and layers of outer clothing from the children. Voices from the living room told us they had all come upstairs. I could hear Amy, and Walter, and an inarticulate murmur from Sandy.

"You go on in there with them, Daisy," said Mrs. Vinton. "I'm free till dinner. What dinner they'll want."

When I came into the living room, I saw Amy on the sofa, holding Sandy in front of her against her knees. Brushing tears away with her free hand, she was saying, "Why should you want to run away, love? Didn't you know I'd worry? Sandy love, you don't have to be afraid of nobody. Or nothing."

I met Walter's eyes. "Ernest found him only half a mile from the pike. He was heading for Boston."

I became aware of Ernest pacing up and down, looking at none of us.

Walter came and stood beside Sandy. "Amy, let me talk to him."

"Don't you frighten him, hear?" she said fiercely. "Sandy's a good boy, and he didn't do anything wrong!"

"I just want him to tell us what he knows."

I ruffled Sandy's hair. He was trembling as a bird trembles, finding himself held in a human hand.

"You found him."

Frances stood in the doorway, one cheek white, one cheek crushed and red from where she had slept heavily on it. She came into the room unsteadily, and Walter helped her onto the sofa. She said, "Tell me what happened to Jeff, Sandy."

Sandy buried his face in Amy's lap. Amy said thickly, "Let him be. He'll tell you."

Ernest stopped his pacing behind me. I could feel him there, without turning my head. He said, "Maybe Daisy could give us some idea when they got out of bed."

"I . . . have no idea. I thought they went to sleep right away. I must have fallen asleep only a short time after."

"Had Amos and Joan already gone?"

"They left about a half hour before I went to sleep."

His tone was inquisitorial, and I bridled. But I realized that to the Freers I was a stranger. I had come to the house on Amos' invitation, and they had accepted me on his judgment. And trusted me with their children, on Amos' judgment. What did they know of me?

Still, I had not been here when Ronnie drowned or when Moira drank the pesticide. I said almost defiantly, "I locked the door when I went to sleep. I would have heard them unlock it, I'm sure." I would not let myself be intimidated by Ernest.

Sandy spoke muffledly from Amy's lap. "The front door was open when we went out. You were in the kitchen. We heard you washing something up."

I would not even have heard them leave over the sound of the running water.

"All right, Sandy," Walter said heavily, "now we know

when you went out. Now tell us exactly how it happened. The truth now, all of it."

"Tell him, Sandy," Amy whispered, stroking his matted hair.

It was as if we five adults stopped breathing as we waited for his first words.

"We never took our clothes off," he said chokingly. "We fooled Daisy, we got into bed with our clothes on."

"Yes?" Walter said impatiently.

"We even had our jackets in bed with us. And we went down real quiet and took the skates from the hall closet. We was real quiet. And we did just like Mr. Freer said, we got the blankets from the dresser and rolled them up to look like us."

I had never even gone back to their room to check. They had not needed any tricks to fool me last night; I was too dead to the world.

"Was it your idea, Sandy?" Frances said harshly.

Walter shook his head. "What difference does it make?"

Amy cried, "Couldn't you have waited till morning? Didn't you have enough time to play in the daytime?"

Sandy began to sob at her tone. "We thought it would be fun at night! Like Mr. Freer said!"

Involuntarily I glanced up at Ernest. He was still as stone.

Walter said thinly, "So you went out to the pond. Did you see anyone there?"

"I don't know! I don't know!"

"Yes, you do know," said Frances. "You know very well indeed how it happened. And you tell us, Sandy, every bit of it!"

I saw Amy's mouth set. But she only whispered to Sandy, "Tell them, love. Don't be scared."

He fixed his eyes on her face, as if he wanted to shut out the sight of the rest of us.

"We never saw the holes. It didn't look any different than when we were there before. And then I skated right by one, and I saw it, and I yelled to Jeff, but he was on the other side ahead of me, and there was another one there, and he didn't see it, and I heard the splash, and I heard him yell, but when I got there, I grabbed at him, but his hat came off, and he wasn't there anymore!"

I could feel a pounding in the top of my head at the horror of it. None of us spoke: Sandy had made it too terribly sharp for us, the whole scene. The wet weight of his heavy winter clothes, the shock of the icy water, he couldn't have struggled, and if he had drifted at once under the ice. . . .

"Why didn't you run to the house and get help?" said Walter in a dead voice.

I could see the terror on Sandy's face, and I knew the answer. He had been afraid. He was six years old even if he looked like eight, and his thinking was a six-year-old's. He had done something terribly wrong, and his first impulse was to hide. Sandy's mouth was open, but no words came, while his frantic eyes remained fixed in desperation on Amy's face.

"What did you do, love?" whispered Amy.

"I ran back here. I was going to get into bed and pretend I was sleeping and didn't know where Jeff was," he whimpered. "Only the door was locked, so I ran to your room, Ma, and went into bed there."

"And left your best friend in that icy water to die!" cried Frances.

"Mama, Mama!" he screamed. His scream cut through me like a knife. He continued to scream as if he would never stop until Amy picked him up as if he were a baby and ran out of the room with him.

We continued to sit there, transfixed with the tableau of that night as Sandy had pictured it.

It was Walter who broke the silence. "When the hell were those holes cut?" he said.

Frances looked at him. "You're sure they weren't there when you were out there earlier?"

"Positive. You saw the ice, Ernest."

Ernest nodded briefly.

"I suppose anyone could have come out after Thanksgiving dinner, wanting a bit of fun," Walter said, answering himself. "It doesn't take more than a few minutes to saw through. They could have come right after we finished skating and had a few hours of fishing before the kids came down."

None of us spoke. I did not look at Ernest, but I thought of him roaming the grounds last night, after everyone had gone. Had he gone to the pond to see. . . . When he walked away from me earlier, where had he gone? He might have waited until the children had finished skating and then returned. Remembering how they had fished through the ice as children, he might have felt an impulse to recapture the experience. And had forgotten to mark the holes. And could not bring himself to admit it, knowing what Frances would think.

No. My mind rejected the possibility. Ernest would have admitted to sawing those holes if it had been carelessness.

And if it had been deliberate?

Strangely, I found myself more ready to believe him a murderer than a liar.

It was nearly ten that night before Amos and Joan returned. I had been watching for their car. When it turned up the drive, I ran downstairs to open the door for them.

They both looked as shaken and exhausted as I had known they would be.

"Help Joan get into bed, Daisy, please. I'm going to see Frances."

We used Mr. Freer's elevator rather than subject her to the stairs. I took her to the door of her bedroom and waited outside until she called me. Joan had an almost puritanical shyness about dressing or undressing in front of me. She was in her gown and robe and in bed when she finally let me come in. I brought her some brandy, and she took it gratefully.

"Pull the drapes, Daisy."

She hated the look of the night outside her windows. I pulled closed the flower-sprigged drapes. She sipped the brandy and shuddered. "Will you light the fire, too?"

The room was warm, almost too warm, as so many New England houses are, but the cold was inside her where the warmth of the room could not reach. I touched a match to the neatly laid wood that Minna always left for them; the spills of paper caught, and then the thin sticks of kindling, the sap on the logs blazed and spat, and the room was bright. Color came into her face, or maybe it was just a reflection from the flames.

"You have to tell me how it happened, Daisy. I know he drowned. Amos told me. I must know how."

There was nothing to conceal, and to hide the details from her was only to arouse her suspicion. "It was an accident," I said dully. Another accident. "Sandy and Jeff went out skating last night, after they pretended to go to bed. Some people must have been ice fishing in the early evening. Jeff didn't see the hole. . . ."

My voice fell away.

"What are you thinking, Daisy?" she said quietly.

"I'm thinking I'm partly to blame," I said, fighting for self-control. "I went to sleep immediately. I should have stayed up and checked on them."

But they had slipped out before I fell asleep. And even if I had checked on them and found them gone, it would have already been too late to save Jeffrey.

I found myself repeating it. "I should have stayed awake and checked them. I don't know why I should have fallen asleep."

"You sound like Amy," she said. "After they found Ronnie."

"But that's nonsense!" I cried. What was she trying to suggest? That I had been drugged? That was the inference she had made about Amy; was it a coincidence that we each had been asleep at the moment that a child died; was it only a coincidence? My mind told me that anyone could have put a pill in something I drank, we were all in the library together for hours, when my senses were not alert.

It could even have been in the coffee that Amos had brought me, that Joan had brewed, if I wanted to be logical.

I fought the idea. "I ate and drank too much, that was all. When I was out at the pond, my head cleared for a while. If I could have stayed out, I would have been better, but it was having nothing to do, the children asleep, the house quiet, no one to talk to—"

"Whatever has happened, Daisy, you mustn't blame yourself. For that matter, Frances had no right to ask you to take care of the children. You weren't here for that reason; you were here to be with me."

"But I did agree to do it—"

"Daisy, you mustn't let this affect you. You have a child within you that needs you well and happy. You have to forget everything but that!"

"How can I, Joan? Even if it weren't that Frances will never forgive me, that I will never be able to face her and Walter, how can I forget poor Jeff? How can I not blame myself?" My voice was rising in spite of my effort to control it. "How can I stay here now? I'll have to go away!"

Her face turned ash gray; even in my own emotional state I saw it. She leaned forward and seized both my hands in a cold, frenzied grip.

"You mustn't think of leaving! You promised Amos!"

Her words to me that first night I came flashed through my mind: *Go away! Don't stay here!* But she had been a stranger then, and neither of us had any idea how close we would become these past months. I said, shaken, "I did promise Amos. But this has changed everything."

"Nothing has changed, for us, for you and me!" she said

passionately. "I need you here, Daisy! I don't think I could stay on in this house if you went away!"

"Of course you could," I said, pressing her cold fingers. "Amos is here."

"No, no! I'd lose my mind!" Her voice was thinning; her eyes looked frantic in her ashen face. "You mustn't let Frances drive you away! You need us as much as we need you. Where will you go? How will you manage, with the baby? Don't go, Daisy. Don't let Frances do this to us. She's done us enough harm already—"

Her anguish brought me to my senses. I mustn't let her break down. It was more than my promise to Amos; it was our debt of friendship to each other. How could I refuse her? I took a deep breath. "I'll stay as long as you want me, Joan."

She let go of my hands and sank back against the pillows, her eyes closed. After a moment she said, "You see, I'll want you here more than ever now. The doctor says I must stay in bed all the time. He says it is a question of whether I'll be able to have the baby at all."

"Oh, Joan." What was there to say? I was too exhausted at this point myself to muster up the words of reassurance.

"Don't tell Frances," she said, her voice unexpectedly hard.

"As if I would."

"I don't want her preening herself over us. She'll find out soon enough she is the only progenitrix of the Freers. The queen bee of the hive." She turned her face bitterly into the pillow.

"I think she'll feel sorry for you," I said, trying to sound convincing even as I remembered Frances' satisfaction when she told me how the coming of Moira had restored her to her father's interest and her place at his side. "She's Amos' sister, and she knows what a child means to you both."

"Daisy, grow up," she said wearily. "Why won't you recognize what she is? She *loves* the idea that hers are the only grandchildren Father will ever have. She *loves* the idea that she's managed to arrange that stock transfer for her children alone."

It took every ounce of energy left in me to rally, for her sake. I even managed a laugh.

"Joan! You're talking as if you've lost the baby! But you haven't! And you won't! Amos and I and you yourself are going to take marvelous care for the next few months, and you're going to have that baby! And you'll be able to face her and think: See, you didn't believe I could make it, but I did!"

She even smiled. A little color came into her face. "Daisy, you're a darling to talk such complete nonsense. But I need that kind of nonsense."

We talked some more, of inconsequential things like the play they'd seen in New York and where they had dined, and I left her only when she was about to drop off to sleep. Her last words to me were, "Thanks, Daisy. For staying. I'll always remember that."

I was too restless to go back to my room. I couldn't watch TV; I had nothing to read; it was too early to go to bed. I thought I might go down to the library and find a book there, but when I went out into the hall, the door to Frances' apartment was open, and I could see them still sitting in her living room, Frances and Walter, Ernest and Amos. Walter looked up and saw me.

"Come in and join us, Daisy," he said heavily.

I had no choice but to go in.

"How is Joan?" Amos said in a low voice.

"Going to sleep."

"Good. I don't know how she survived that drive home."

Amy had packed her things and left with Sandy for good. Cory had driven them to her father's house in Bright River. The family had been discussing Sandy when I came in, and his part in Jeff's death. Only Frances was ready to blame him.

"He was intelligent enough to know what to do. If he had only run for help—"

"Frances, it would have already been too late," said Walter wearily. "That icy water. It would have taken awhile to locate him. Why don't you get that into your head?"

"I hope he died quickly. I hope he didn't suffer," she said, and wept.

Ernest got up from his chair and began to pace. He looked more worn than Walter.

Frances said between sobs, "I knew there was bad blood in that child! What kind of man was his father, to abandon Amy and his child? He must have been a vicious person!"

The room fell into abrupt silence. They were all scrupulously avoiding looking at me. . . .

Ernest said with sudden violence, "Why don't you stop harping on that kid's blood? None of us has blood that's untainted. Mother would have died in an institution if we hadn't been rich enough to keep nurses for her round the clock. Father's been senile for over a year—"

"Father had a stroke!" Frances flared. "That's not being

senile! You're only condemning him because he preferred me to you—"

"If he preferred you to me, it was because you've been working on him," Ernest said. "You've made it your life's work, getting him to prefer you to us!"

"That's enough, Ernest," Walter said, standing up. "I won't have Frances spoken to like that, in her own house. And today, of all days. Where's your decency, man? Or is that too much to expect?"

Ernest fell silent. I could see his face working. "It's too much to expect," he muttered, and strode from the room.

Constraint settled down on us. No one spoke.

It was Amos who broke the silence. "Don't blame him for anything he says today. This must have brought it all back to him, the day Ronnie died."

"As a matter of fact, he's been unusually decent today," Walter said. "He ran to get help; he stayed with us through the whole nightmare of this morning. It was Ernest who found Sandy. I thought it was remembering Ronnie that made him as sympathetic as he was."

"Do you honestly believe he's sympathetic toward us?" Frances said bitterly. "I can't remember a time when he hasn't been full of hate for us, not since the day he brought that woman into the house!"

Walter shook his head warningly at Amos, as if asking him not to contradict her.

Amos said, "The one I pity is Sandy."

"Sandy!" Frances cried, outraged. "I'll never forgive him!"

"What I'm afraid of," said Amos levelly, "is that he may

never forgive himself. And that's too much of a burden for a child."

"It's easy to be charitable when it isn't your child lying dead," she flung at him.

I saw him flinch, and I wanted to defend him, but I didn't feel up to having the brunt of her venom directed at me. I rose. "I think I'll go to bed," I said without looking at any of them, and left.

Amos caught me as I reached the door of my room.

"Daisy."

I turned.

"Don't mind Frances too much. She's stupid, and often she's cruel."

"I really don't mind her too much," I said. "It's just that today—"

He reached out and rubbed my cheek with the back of his hand. "Don't let her frighten you."

I don't know exactly how it happened, whether he leaned forward to kiss me good-night, something he had never done before but which he was moved to do out of our low spirits, or whether the horror of the day had filled me with the terrible need to be close to someone, and I moved first. But suddenly my head was pressed into his shoulder and his arms were around me.

It was painful to step away. I did not want him to see how deeply stirred I was, and I moved back hurriedly into the darkness of my room.

"Forgive me for that," he said. "It won't happen again."

Later when I lay in bed too restless for sleep, I thought: It mustn't happen again.

IV

1

M**R. FREER CONTINUED** to ask for Jeffrey queru-
lously, but obeying Frances' orders, we kept up a myth that
Jeffrey was in the hospital for an appendectomy.

The words stuck in my throat, and I knew what a terrible
effort was required of Frances each time she said, "He's
coming along nicely, Father." But the need to protect her
father must have been almost as strong as her grief for
Jeffrey; else how could she have kept up the fiction?

But with Dr. Raab standing by, at last Mr. Freer was
told. He took the news better than anyone expected, but
then perhaps he did not completely comprehend it. "Where
is Sandy?" he said fretfully. "Did he drown, too?"

"He's living in town with Amy now, Father."

Mr. Freer shook his head slowly. "Jeffrey is a fine boy.
And Sandy, too. All . . . all fine boys."

He must have understood more than we realized, however, because a change seemed to come over him. On Friday
nights when we all dined together, he hardly spoke to any

of us, sunk in himself, having to be roused even to eat his food.

The Friday night dinner had become a trial to me, now that Joan no longer came to the table, and finally I prevailed on Amos to let me have my dinner with Joan in her room.

She was growing paler and thinner. The size of her baby was more marked than mine because of her slightness; mine was still not too noticeable under the loose tops of my jumpers. But it was not her slightness that disturbed me or even her pallor—how could she have color in her face, cooped up in that overheated room all day?—it was her growing despondency. She had lost interest in everything. She did not want to be distracted by games or light talk, and there was a kind of hopelessness in her glance.

I was almost embarrassed by my own well-being, which even overcame the oppressiveness and tension in the house. I went for walks whenever I could, usually while Joan napped or on the days when I left her to Amos. There was always snow on the ground now, and I did not venture to walk on the perilous cliff walk even in daylight. Still, the ocean tugged, and I would walk as far as the snow fence and stare down at its metallic surface, marked occasionally by a fishing boat which left a V of white water in its wake and a swarm of pursuing gulls.

When I met Ernest near the cliffs, we would nod briefly but not speak. I wondered often why Julia had not loved him enough to stay here. If he had been happy, and there was a time when he must have been, he would be an attractive man, in a quiet way, and it was Amos' quiet way that had first drawn me to him. Or had that anger I sensed been too close to the surface, even with her? I would not want that anger directed against me.

I only left the house to shop or visit Dr. Raab. Until now Joan or Frances had driven me to Bright River, but now Joan stayed in bed, and I didn't want to ask Frances. She had begun to soften toward me, even making gruff overtures of conversation. I think she might even have missed the talks we once had. Still when it was time for my appointment with Dr. Raab, I asked Amos if I might not ride in with him in the morning.

"Sure, Daisy. Can you wait until lunchtime to go home?"

I didn't mind. I could use the time to do some Christmas shopping, just small things, for the children. And I wanted to buy something for Sandy.

Walter came with us in the morning, and they dropped me at Dr. Raab's house, with its delicately constructed widow's walk on the roof.

"Shall I pick you up here or in town?"

I said, "Pick me up at Amy's house. I might stop in and see how she is."

"That would be nice. See you around noon then."

Dr. Raab was pleased with me. He told me my rambles were all right as long as I didn't get too tired, and prescribed more vitamins, and made an appointment for next month.

The local drugstore was also a general store, and I was able to buy a paint set for Sandy and a small bottle of cologne for Amy. I had heard through Minna that she was not working, and I knew how hard it would be for her to buy necessities, let alone luxuries. I also found some doll-sized furniture for Maggie's collection of dolls and some blocks for Moira. With my packages in a shopping bag, I walked down the old street that ended at the wharfs and found Amy's house.

The house needed painting; the steps sagged. Two ancient lilac bushes at each side of the path wore hoods of snow. I went up the steps carefully and rang the bell.

Sandy answered the door. The smile on his face faded when he saw me. "Ma!" he yelled, and ran down the long narrow hall that bisected the house from front to back.

He came back behind Amy, who looked coldly suspicious, but she invited me into a dim little parlor where a black sofa that looked as if no one had ever sat on it stood between two small tables covered with pots of fern. She motioned me to sit down, and I did, on the unyielding horsehair cushions of the sofa. The room was musty and hot.

"Isn't Sandy going to school?" I asked, surprised to find him home. "Oh, I forgot. He goes in the afternoon."

"I don't go anymore," said Sandy.

Amy interposed quickly, "He's had a cold."

He didn't look as if he had a cold, but he did look different. The Sandy I remembered stood square, self-assured, with unclouded eyes. This Sandy watched me furtively, pressed against his mother's side.

The unfriendliness in the room was tangible. Maybe Amy blamed me, too, like Frances. If I had not fallen asleep that night, she would still be living with Sandy at the Freers', earning a decent salary, wearing Julia's fine made-over clothes. Or maybe she only associated me with the Freers, and I came in for her anger against them. I could understand her coldness, and I wondered what I could do to restore the old relationship between us.

"How is your father?" I asked, to break the silence.

"Okay. Working. He's at the freezer plant. Works for Freers, like everybody else in town."

Silence. I tried again. "You dropped out of sight so completely. I was sure we'd see each other again."

She said bitterly, "I'll never go near that house again."

"Amy, we all have to forget what happened. No one blamed you. If they blamed anybody, it was me."

"The way they talked to him." She stopped, glancing down quickly at Sandy. He was listening hard, his mouth open. She shook her head at me, warning me.

I thought of what Dr. Raab had told me that day, and I repeated his words. "We shouldn't hold anything she said at the time against her. I might have acted worse. Or you, Amy."

She conceded the possibility grudgingly.

"I know they miss you." Frances had said that just the other day. The new girl they had hired, Matthilde, was clumsy and slow, without Amy's intelligence.

Again her glance darted toward Sandy. "How could we ever live there, *now*?"

I could understand her feelings. All the places where Sandy had played with Jeff, the nursery, the maze, the barns, and not just the pond, would keep a terrible memory green in his mind. The damage was done to him already, and who could tell yet how deep it was?

"Anyway, I don't like her," she said, of Frances. "She's a cold one. I could tell when Ronnie died. She didn't really care, for all the proper things she said at the proper times. Only one she cares about is Mr. Freer, and that because he's the one with the power. And the money. She'd like to take over if she could, take over everything. If you ask me, she's stronger than both her brothers, stronger even than Mr. Ernest for all he scares you."

It was hard to deny it.

"She needed every bit of that strength," I said, "to get through these last weeks."

She was studying me. "Didn't it ever strike you as queer, Daisy, two children dying the way they did?"

"It struck me as tragic, when they might have been prevented," I said. "Like all accidents."

She said slowly, "They seem real queer to me."

"Oh, not you too, Amy. You sound like Joan."

She looked down at Sandy. "You cleaned up your room yet, Sandy?"

"I will," he muttered. "Later."

"*Now*," she said sharply. "Go clean it now."

He went off with a meekness I did not remember in him before. It was as if his spirit was quenched.

She waited until we could hear his door close down the hall, and then she said, "Everybody in town's been talking about how it happened." The blood surged up into her cheeks. "Those holes in the ice weren't there to begin with, and any men come over from the town to fish would have known enough to put up markers where they were. My dad talks to lots of people in Bright River, and nobody knows anybody that went up to the Cove that night to fish."

"They could have come from another town."

"Sure they could," she said contemptuously. "And who'd go to the trouble to saw those holes for just an hour or two? They'd have planned to stay most of the night, and they'd have been there when the boys came down to skate."

"What are you saying, Amy?" But I knew what she was saying.

"I'm saying it was someone in the family did it, and did it because they wanted to get Jeff. And they didn't even care if they got Sandy, too, at the same time, just so they'd get Jeff."

"No, Amy!"

"You don't want to admit it any more than they do. But you know it was Ernest did it."

I shook my head, trying to find some words of conviction, but the suspicion was too strong in my own mind, too. "And Ronnie?" I said. "Surely you're not suggesting he killed his own child!"

"Could have been Frances killed Ronnie," she said darkly. "And Ernest killed her boy, to get even."

"I won't believe that," I said, shaking my head. "If you remind me that Ernest is . . . was . . . sick and could have done it because he was sick, I could understand it, even if I didn't believe it. But I won't believe it of Frances. Why?"

"Money," she said. "All the money in that trust fund they're always squabbling about goes to her own children."

"But there's plenty to go around!"

She cried, "She hated Ronnie! I could see the way she acted to her! Hated the mother, hated the child!"

I turned away. "Maybe she hated her, but not enough to kill her."

"Believe what you want," she said. "Are you saying it wasn't queer the way you went to sleep? It was queer the way *I* went to sleep, and that's a fact. I never fell asleep with the children before. Or after."

I said firmly, "I drank too much."

"Well, I never drank nothing but milk," she said. "*She* knew I always had milk with the children before I took them outside. She could have put something in it."

"She wasn't even in Freer's Cove when it happened, Amy! She'd taken Maggie and Jeff and Sandy to Bright River!"

"Did any one of us notice when she went? Or when she came back? We didn't find Ronnie for hours later, and no one would think to ask any of the family."

I continued to shake my head. "I can't see Frances as a murderer. Killing implies a sick mind, and she isn't sick."

"How do you know she isn't sick?" she demanded. "Because she acts okay? Ernest acts okay now, too. Just because they have all that money and their name is Freer, you think they can't be sick?"

I shook my head.

"Money makes people crazy sometimes, when they want it bad enough!"

"I don't believe Ernest gives a damn about the money."

"That wasn't his reason," she said, scornful of my stupidity. "Ernest did it to get even. On one of his walks he could have dropped the poison where the children could get at it. He didn't care which one, so long as it was one of hers, and maybe he even figured it wouldn't be Sandy because Sandy was too smart to drink it."

"The skating was clearly an accident," I said firmly.

"The boys came back from dinner full of talk of what went on when Ernest and Amos were boys. They thought it was great, how they'd sneak out at night. And those blankets. I heard them going on. I tell you even if Ernest didn't cut those holes, even if Jeff didn't get drowned that night, he'd have found some other way to get at him, some other time."

I'm as familiar with murders as most people: I read about them in newspapers and books, I see them on television and in the movies. But I have never seen a murder, or known a murderer, that I know of, and so my mind can comprehend murder about the way it can comprehend space exploration. I accept it, I know it's possible and has been done, but I don't really understand how it works. I know it's naïve, but there it is. I can see how Ernest, deranged with grief, might harbor the seeds of murder. But not Frances, surely. . . . And yet there was their mother, and the same blood runs in their veins.

"Anyway, it's none of my business anymore, and I'm glad," she said. "Let them kill each other off if they want; it don't matter to me anymore. Just let them keep my Sandy out of it. They've done him enough harm already, everybody in town pointing a finger at him."

"Oh, *no*, Amy," I said, shocked. "You're imagining it."

"Why don't I let him go to school then, if I'm only imagining it? Kids keep asking him why he let Jeff drown. They even asked Sandy if he pushed him in. Teacher told me. They hear talk at home." There were tears in her eyes.

I put my hand on her arm. "Amy, don't. It will all blow over soon enough. People have short memories. And anyone who knows Sandy wouldn't believe anything bad of him. Even the Freers have accepted it as an accident."

"Was no accident," she said stubbornly. "Those holes were no accident. Someone sneaking over to the pond and sawing them, hoping that a kid would drown in them. Sandy screams in the middle of the night now. My father complains he can't get any sleep, but how can I stop Sandy from dreaming bad dreams? Sandy knows something bad happened that night, something . . . evil."

I knew she was indulging her bitterness against the Freers for blaming Sandy. I knew she was brooding the long days at home and using her imagination to clothe the facts, but her words sent a chill through me anyway. Resolutely I produced my shopping bag and brought out my packages in their red and silver wrappings.

"Amy, won't you put these under the tree, for you and Sandy?"

She reddened with pleasure. "You shouldn't have, Daisy. You'll be needing your money." She put the gifts into the bottom drawer of a nearby chest, and when she spoke again, it was more on our old footing. "Just you keep your eyes open in that house, is all I say."

We talked until the front doorbell rang.

"That must be Amos." I put on my coat, and we went out into the hall. I raised my voice. "So long, Sandy!" But he didn't answer. Maybe he didn't hear me.

Amy opened the door. It was not Amos, but Ernest who stood on the porch. Amy looked disconcerted.

"How are you, Amy?" he said. He did not look like a murderer in his plaid mackinaw and fur hat, but then what do murderers look like? "I've come to take Miss Holland back. Amos is involved at the office and won't be coming home. How's Sandy?"

She swallowed. "We're both okay, thanks."

"I'm ready," I said to him, and to Amy, "Come and see me, soon."

"One of these days. Maybe," she said.

The snow had hardened into deep ruts, making walking uncertain, and he took my arm to help me into the car. He always avoided looking at me, or speaking to me, for that matter, any more than was necessary. After our words at the pond I no longer even tried to make conversation with him, and we rode in silence almost to the private road before he surprised me by saying, "Is Sandy all right?"

"He's changed. She doesn't let him go to school anymore, because the children tease him."

He said, after a minute, "I figured it would be like that, in a place like Bright River."

We drove through the gates. They were always open during the day, and often at night if Cory forgot to close them. Cory was the only one who might spot an intruder, and his sight and hearing were dulled by age. Besides, if anyone chose to poach on Freer land, there were acres of open field through which entrance could be made, unseen.

He pulled up at the front steps but continued to sit, frowning at nothing. I certainly did not need or expect his help in getting out of the car. Still, it was unfriendly and surly, his not even making a move. I put my hand on the door handle.

He said, not turning his head, "You still insist on staying here." It wasn't a question.

They were almost the words he had used that first night I had come here. This time I said calmly enough, "I made an agreement with Amos. To stay on until Joan's baby, and my own, were born."

"It can't be a pleasant place for you."

"For anyone, when a child dies," I said steadily.

"Then why don't you leave? You may be in danger here."

I said, trying to maintain the same steadiness, "Why should anyone want to hurt me?"

He looked fully at me, one of those rare times. "You know you're scared. Go home, for God's sake."

I opened the car door. "I made an agreement, and I intend to stick to it."

I went into the house and up to our rooms. But a thought came to me: He doesn't want me here because I am an outsider, and privy to the family secrets. The family might protect him if they knew he were guilty, but why should I? How much would I betray, if I had to? Was that why I was in danger? Was that why he was so openly hostile to me? Might I, for instance, speculate too closely on where Julia was?

2

Christmas came.

It was painful to prepare for a holiday that was so bound up with the children; I know we all were oppressed with memories of Jeff and Ronnie. It would be the first Christmas without them. Frances made a heroic effort to have the decorations brought down so she could begin trimming the tree. Cory and Sam had set it up in the living room, and we all helped Frances hang the ornaments. I suppose she was most concerned that old Mr. Freer have his usual holiday, but it was a silent evening.

Maggie had been allowed to stay up a little later, because Frances and Walter thought that trimming the tree might cheer her up. She missed Jeff, and Sandy, too, I suppose, more than any of us imagined a four-year-old could. Now she held out a Santa Claus soberly to her mother.

"Mommy, can I hang Jeff's Santa Claus?"

"Sure," said Frances shortly, averting her face.

I'd had the idea earlier to bring Joan down into the living room for the tree trimming. She too seemed to grow increasingly despondent with the onset of Christmas, and I hoped it might distract her to be with us all.

"Amos can carry you down, Joan."

She looked at Amos, almost as if she asked permission.

"Why not?" he said. "I'll wrap you in a quilt, and you can sit on the big chair near the fire."

She let me fuss with her hair and even added lipstick herself, and Amos carried her down, her slender neck and blue-veined wrists showing beyond the ruffles of her robe. No doubt the doctor knew what was best for her when he confined her to her bed, but I wondered if he were aware of the harm he had done her psychologically.

After Matthilde had taken Maggie upstairs to bed, Sam brought in a tray of well-spiked eggnog and small cakes. We all had some, even Mr. Freer, huddled in his wheelchair, only now and then lifting his eyes to stare at the tree. Frances hovered over him, talking brightly. Ernest surprised us by sitting beside Joan, as if he sensed a despondency in her almost like his own.

I sat near Amos.

"When will you be going in to see her doctor again? Joan said it was up to you; you were very tied up just now."

"It will have to be after New Year's," he said. "Some bankers are coming up from Boston to inspect the plant. We're still trying to finance the expansion without selling any more stock, and money is too tight. Why?"

"I think you should explain to the doctor what's happening to Joan. Maybe he'll relent and let her out for part of the day at least. She doesn't look at all well."

A furrow appeared between his brows. "Don't even suggest the possibility to her, Daisy. I know from the way the doctor spoke the last time that this is a last-ditch hope. She's got to do everything possible for her own sake. God knows what would happen to her if she lost this baby."

"She would want to try again, just as you would, Amos. People have reserves of hope in them. How could we get through life without them?"

He patted my hand. "You're very encouraging, Daisy." He even smiled, making me feel as if I had sounded like a child with my foolish optimism. "I often wonder if we haven't been unfair to you, saddling you with all our problems."

"But I want to feel I'm of use to you!" I said with fervor. I don't know what made me look up at that moment, unless I had felt someone's eyes on me. It was Ernest, his glance appraising. I became aware of how close Amos and I were sitting, our heads together so as to speak without being overheard; he might even have seen that quick pat of Amos' hand. Involuntarily I made a move away, and spilled eggnog on my skirt, and had to take myself off to the small pantry adjoining to sponge off the stain. I was more disturbed than usual by Ernest's watching us. It was not his hostility, which I was used to by now, but something else. Did I unconsciously seek these moments alone with Amos; did I want his compliments, his sympathy; did I want them more than I had any right to? It was as if Ernest's look had seen what I hadn't seen myself.

When I came back again into the living room, Ernest was gone. Mr. Freer was asleep, and Frances signaled Sam to wheel her father to his room.

The five of us were left. Frances said suddenly, "Walter wants me to fly to Kip's Bay with him for a week. He thinks it will do me good."

"Why don't you, Frances?" Joan said with unexpected animation. "How I wish I could go, go anywhere at all!"

"She doesn't want to leave the children," said Walter glumly.

"Take them with you, why don't you?" Amos said.

"It'd hardly be a vacation with them," Walter said.

"And we would have to take Matthilde," Frances said. "Do you know what the rates are in Kip's Bay, in high season? Simply outrageous."

"Oh, come on, Frances, you can afford it," Amos said.

"What's the point of a vacation with children?" Walter interposed again, before Frances could make the sharp retort I was sure she was about to. "It isn't just a change of scene Frances needs, it's a complete change of outlook, and she isn't going to get it with the children around her."

"Why shouldn't you leave them at home?" I said. "You have Matthilde, and Mrs. Vinton, and the rest of us here—" I said it without thinking. The silence that followed my words was uncomfortable, and I realized suddenly what was in their minds. What good did your all being here do for poor Jeff?

Frances said evenly, "I don't like to leave them with . . . with Ernest in the house."

"Now, Frances," Walter said, looking unhappy.

"You needn't try and stop me. They may as well know how I feel. I don't trust Ernest!"

"Joan, you look ready for bed," Amos said.

She met his eyes mutely.

Without another word he gathered her up in his arms and carried her away. When I started to follow, he called over his shoulder, "You stay there, Daisy. I can manage."

I sat down uncomfortably. I still did not feel entirely at ease with Frances, I felt she had not completely forgiven me for my part in Jeffrey's death, and now her accusing words made me feel I should not be here to listen to them.

Walter too seemed jolted by her outburst. "Try and be more careful what you say in front of Joan."

"Joan, Joan," said Frances sullenly. "I'm sick and tired of all the fuss that's made over her. Anyone would think it was the only baby to be born in this house."

Her glance flickered over me defiantly: Tell Joan what I said. I don't care.

"It might very well be the last baby to be born here," Walter said soberly.

I looked up. "What about Ernest? He might marry again."

"Never," Frances said shortly. "That woman ruined his life. Look what she did to him, look what she made him into."

A murderer, said her look.

Walter shifted the conversation. "I thought Father looked a bit more animated when he talked to Joan. I heard him say he hoped it would be a boy. I wonder if he realizes that as of now there are no Freers to carry on the name, I wonder if he thinks about Joan's baby as the heir to the name."

He was thoughtless. Frances' nostrils whitened.

"All this fuss in this day and age about a boy!" she flared. "Really, does anyone in 1971 believe there is any difference in competence between the sexes? My father lives in the days of his childhood; he hasn't changed a bit! Why, I remember when he wouldn't let me down to the Fisheries because he thought man talk was too strong for my ears! Why, I could cuss as well as any man!"

"Still a few jobs you couldn't cope with, Frances," said her husband with a clumsy attempt at teasing. "Do you think you could go out on the boats as Ernest does, in all kinds of weather, ankle-deep in bloody fish guts—"

"And when was the last time he went out on the boats?" she said venomously.

"Last week," Walter said.

She snorted.

"I think it's a good sign," Walter said. "I think it means he's definitely out of the rough."

She burst out, clearly indifferent to the extent of Ernest's recovery, "It's plain as day that Joan isn't strong enough to bear a child. I'm surprised at Amos. He's so madly in love with her, and yet he subjects her again and again to danger. He must be aware this baby could kill her."

"Frances, if the doctor didn't think she could go through with it, he wouldn't have allowed it to go so far," Walter said.

"Nor would Amos have allowed it." I had to say it. I knew Amos and Joan, I felt, better than any of them by this time.

The conversation ended suddenly when Amos came in. He said at once, as if there had been no interruption when he had carried Joan away, "I know how you feel about Ernest,

Frances, but I'd appreciate it if you'd keep such talk to yourself, especially in front of Joan."

"It's more than just a case of how I feel," she said tightly. "You know you all feel the same way. My child is dead. How long are we supposed to keep our suspicions to ourselves? Does another child have to die?"

The silence was uncomfortable. She had already said too much in front of me, and they all were clearly aware of it. I stood up. "I think I'll read in my room for a while."

Amos said, "I think now you'd better stay, Daisy. You've heard this much, and in fairness to Ernest you should hear how the rest of us feel. Frances made what amounted to an accusation. To me, the thought is preposterous."

"You call it a preposterous accusation when I can't leave my own children in my own house and be sure they will be safe? Two deaths in less than a year. What might have been a fatal poisoning. Preposterous?" Her voice had risen shrilly.

Amos' mind worked as mine had, with Amy. "Are you suggesting that Ernest killed his own daughter?"

"You don't think it's possible?" she demanded. "Julia drove him out of his mind. I can see him doing it to hurt her."

"Ernest would have killed anyone that laid a hand on Ronnie." He stopped and flushed. *Ernest would have killed.* It was precise, careful, unimpassioned Amos who had said it.

But he was going on. "Why is it so hard to see that both children died accidentally? I call Joan neurotic when she says what you say. You're supposed to be level-headed. Come now, show me that you're more sensible than that. In both cases we know how it happened, more or less. Wouldn't we be a lot happier if we let things lie that way?"

"Amos is right," Walter said. "You were ready enough to believe Ronnie's death was an accident, but now you're calling them both murder." He looked uncomfortable as he said the word.

"He's sick," she said in a low voice, looking up at the door as if she were afraid Ernest might return. "You know he is. The doctors called it a nervous breakdown. They said in time they hoped he would recover. In time. What time? They *hoped* he would recover. They didn't know for sure; they only hoped. Don't call me neurotic, Amos. You're just not willing to face the facts. You never could. You were always looking for another way."

"Amos isn't saying Ernest isn't sick, Fran," her husband said. "He's only saying that he isn't a murderer. The good Lord knows how hard he's been pressed, losing an only child. And that bitch of a wife—But then he loved her, and losing her pushed him over the deep end. But that doesn't make him a murderer, Fran."

Frances cried, "I wish I could be as sure as you are!"

Walter sat down beside her and slipped his arm around her shoulders. "You need a vacation, old girl; that's what you need. I'm going to put my foot down for once and insist that you take one. I'll call Byers in the morning and tell him to make the reservations. And if you back out, just watch it, Fran, I might have to find someone to take your place."

His forced heartiness didn't fool anyone. He too was shaken by her conviction.

Frances slipped out of his hold, unmollified.

"Let's set out the damned presents, and then I'm going to bed," she said thickly.

We all scattered to our rooms, to return with the presents,

incongruously festive in their gilt wrappers and red ribbons. Walter wheeled over a small bike, for Maggie.

"Jeffrey used to be the first one down on Christmas morning," Frances said, and suddenly burst into tears.

"All right, old girl, all right, my dear," Walter said, and led her out of the room.

Amos and I were shaken by her tears and looked at each other bleakly.

"Still, she's heroic, the way she holds on to herself most of the time," I said. "I wonder if I could."

He burst out, "Why does she have to attack Ernest? It was so clearly an accident!"

"Because he does seem to hate her."

"And why not? She gave Julia a rough time. And because she disliked Julia, she couldn't show any warmth even to Ronnie."

"I can see why he couldn't forgive her, but—"

He wasn't listening to me, staring broodingly into the fire. "Ernest is right when he says there's a weak strain in the Freers. We can't take too much stress. I wonder sometimes—" He stopped and looked at me as if he were uncertain whether to finish, but he went on: "I wonder how much more I can take."

"Don't talk like that!" I cried. "You mustn't. What would they all do without you? Joan—why, she'd go to pieces if it weren't for you!"

"And you." He smiled crookedly. "I'm just indulging myself, begging for a little sympathy. You have to admit it's been a lot to take. Not just Joan and the worry about the baby. But Ronnie and Jeff. And Ernest. And the business has been milked almost to the limit. Oh, I suppose it will go on forever, even without the freezer plant, but it's so plainly what we need. She should have seen, Frances, that—Well, it's over, and my father has crippled us by taking out so much stock. I did want to—" He clamped his mouth shut, was silent, and then smiled that transforming smile. "It's wonderful having you to talk to, Daisy."

I swallowed. This is where it must stop. I rose firmly.

"I guess I'd better get some sleep."

"I'll come up with you."

Unconsciously, as we went upstairs, he took my hand. I let him, it was a casual gesture, and tonight he seemed to need it. We had just reached the landing when the front door opened and Ernest came in. He stared up at us. I drew my hand away, but he must have seen us. I wished he hadn't.

"Merry Christmas," Ernest said dryly.

Amos was oblivious. "Is it that late already?" he said absently. "Merry Christmas."

3

Joan must have found the diversion of leaving her room last night pleasant, and in the morning it was she who asked Amos to take her down to watch the children open their presents.

The children. There were only two now, with even Sandy gone. And Moira could still do nothing more but scratch at the wrappings. For Moira there was as much interest in tearing the paper off her gifts as in the gifts themselves. She laughed when we laughed and then dropped her toys to prac-

tice her newest accomplishment, tottering from one out-
stretched hand to another.

Mr. Freer was delighted with her; he had his chair
wheeled where he could watch her. For the rest of the family there was a nod and a tendering of his cheek to be
kissed as he received each gift, the clock-radio, the mono-
grammed robe, the handsome book about ships.

Maggie seemed pleased with my dollhouse furniture,
though it paled beside the bike and the white fur coat from
Mr. Freer. And to my embarrassment I was remembered by
everyone in the family, but then, so I discovered, were the
other servants. There was even a pair of fur-lined gloves
from Ernest, which stunned me until I remembered how
Frances had grumbled last week about having to do Ernest's
shopping for him. There was a compact from Frances, a
beautiful evening bag from Joan and Amos, a wallet from
Mr. Freer. In spite of myself, I was excited, caught up in the
pleasure of receiving pretty new things.

Ernest did not appear at all. I found myself looking for
him, wondering at myself a little as I did. He plainly did
not share Frances' drive to maintain the family tradition, for
the sake of Maggie and Moira, but especially, I think, for
Mr. Freer; certainly he didn't seem to have the stomach to
go through that morning, with Ronnie gone.

At last every gift was opened and exclaimed over, the
last wrappings picked off the floor by Mrs. Vinton, and the
false elation died away. We were left without the semblance
of activity to camouflage the terrible sense of loss. I wished
Joan would ask to get back to her room, I wanted to go with
her, when just then there was a tap on the door, and Sam
looked in and beckoned to Amos.

Amos left, closing the door behind him. We all stared after him. He was back in a moment, holding in his hand a covered basket. He knelt down beside Maggie.

"Did you think Santa forgot your gift from Aunt Joan and me?"

She stared at him.

"His messenger was late, delivering this. He hopes you'll forgive him."

He uncovered the basket with a flourish. The thin yelping from inside was almost drowned out by Maggie's excited shriek. For a few moments she could only clap her hands and jump up and down, speechless, pale with joy and surprise. Amos pulled out a small brown and white spotted dog, and put it in her arms.

"Mommy, look," Maggie whispered, holding the dog as if it might shatter in her hands.

"Joan, it was the nicest idea," I said to her.

"Amos thought of it," she said, pleased. "He said it would make Maggie less lonesome."

Even Frances was touched. She stood up and kissed Amos and Joan. "If Walter and I had been thinking a little more clearly these days, we might have come up with it ourselves."

"It's odd, there not being a dog in this big house," I said.

There was a pause, and then Walter said to me, in an undertone, "There hasn't been a dog here since Ann died. She'd had a dog, and after she died, they never had another. So as not to upset Mrs. Freer. I don't think Father would have minded. See, he's probably forgotten already."

Mr. Freer had stretched out his good hand and was patting the dog's head.

"What is his name, Maggie?"

She couldn't understand his slurred speech, and Frances had to tell her what he had said. "Grandpa wants to know what you are going to name him."

"Brownie," said Maggie, without hesitation, as if it were the only possible name.

The morning slipped by almost happily. By late afternoon it began to snow, thickly, sweeping against the windows in a solid sheet of cotton batting. At first I was as delighted as Maggie, and while Joan napped, I went outside to watch the children on the sleds, Matthilde holding Moira, while Maggie coasted behind her. I wished I were not so cumbersome; I wished I could have joined them.

The snow continued that weekend without letup, the drifts growing too deep for walking. The sky stayed continuously gray, and the atmosphere began to grow oppressive. It was as if we were being buried in snow; there was no more exhilaration. Temperatures dropped; a thick ice glaze covered the fields. The men went to work on Monday in snowmobiles, Amos and Ernest in one, Walter in another. I watched them leave in a furious explosion of noise, and again I envied them and fretted about being confined to the house.

But the confinement finally pushed Frances and Walter on their holiday. She had grown restless, even coming into Joan's bedroom to sit with us, not entirely welcome to either of us. She only served as a reminder to Joan, who would study Frances' face now and then in silence, as if she were probing to detect the marks of grief. She kept talking about how wonderful it would be to get away to the south and the sun, and I could see Joan's mouth tighten with longing. It did not take any urging from either of us, but rather the weather finally drove her and Walter to pack their bags and take off for their week at Kip's Bay. Joan promised to postpone her doctor's visit to New York until they were back, and Amos drove them to the airport for their plane.

At that point I think I would have been appeased just to get out of the house. I am an outdoor girl, and I wilt like a flower out of water when I'm kept indoors too long. I had to satisfy myself with moving about the big house, playing now and then with Moira and Maggie and Brownie or reading in the library, which would be cheerfully lit when Mr. Freer was not there.

New snow fell on top of the glaze, but walking was still dangerous. I peered out the window at the playground, which could no longer be used. Only the gaunt witch of the sliding pond and the tops of the yew maze were visible. Joan must have read my thoughts.

"You're not used to this, are you, Daisy? You must be terribly bored."

"Not really," I lied halfheartedly.

"I'll ask Amos to take you to the movies tonight."

I said hastily, "I wouldn't dream of it. Saturday night belongs to the two of you."

Amos had wandered in. "What's this?"

"Poor Daisy feels snowbound. It isn't fair that she has to put up with it. Why don't you take her to the movies, darling?"

"I'd be glad to," he said. "I was planning on a fast game of canasta with you."

"And that's exactly what you're going to do," I said. "Are any of the servants going to Bright River? I might get a lift one way and take a taxi back."

"Let me ask Ernest if he's going into town. He sometimes spends Saturday night at Canuck's Bar."

"Oh, don't ask him, please!" I said. Joan looked at me. Had I revealed too plainly that I didn't want to be alone with him?

She said, "Are you afraid of Ernest, Daisy?"

"Not *afraid*, Joan. Why should I be afraid?" I tried to sound as if I meant it, for her sake, or I would only confirm her fears. And I wanted to, for my own sake, too. I wanted so much to believe there was no reason to be afraid. "But I don't want him put into a position where he can't refuse. He isn't exactly eager for my company."

"He can't object to a ten-minute drive in your company," Amos said. "Let me ask him. He's generally at loose ends when he isn't at the plant."

He must have seen Ernest sometime during the afternoon and spoken to him, and Ernest must have delayed answering him, because we were just having coffee at the dinner table when there was a knock on the outer door. I went to answer it, and it was Ernest.

"I plan to drive into town around eight, if you want to come along. I think the show goes on around eight thirty."

To refuse at this point would be churlish. "I'd like to, yes. Thanks."

Amos said to me when he had gone, "You mustn't be affected by what Frances thinks, Daisy. Ernest is coming along nicely, and there's no reason to be afraid of him. And no reason to connect him with anything that happened here."

"It isn't so much that I'm afraid of him. But he doesn't like me, and it makes me uncomfortable with him."

He said, "You may remind him too much of Julia."

He, too, saw a resemblance. Joan was calling petulantly from the bedroom, "Come in here and talk!" and we went into her bedroom.

Amos repeated what he had told me. "That could be the reason for his disliking her, if Daisy is right that he does."

"As if Daisy were anything like Julia," Joan said. "I think you may have prejudiced him by wearing that red coat and reminding him of her."

But he had disliked me from the first, before I had even seen Julia's coat.

"I never understood his infatuation with Julia," Amos was saying. "She was handsome enough, but all that makeup — If she'd have been my wife, I'd have made her wash her face. I think she was the first girl he ever had, and she bowled him over."

And he had loved her passionately, for all her makeup. I could imagine how she must have swept through this somber great house of the Freers, too gaudy, too volatile, too coarse, too alive. Maybe he had loved her as he did because it seemed so unlikely that he should ever possess anyone like her. Her absence must have left a vast desolation in him, like a bright light going out. No wonder he wandered the estate as if he had lost his bearings. I was stirred with sudden pity. It seemed not hard to pity him when I was not face to face with his open hostility.

I had to wear her coat that night; it was the only one I had that was voluminous enough to cover me completely. To confound any memory of Julia I pulled a knitted cap down over my ears in a way that clothes-conscious Julia would never have tolerated and went downstairs to meet Ernest.

He was waiting for me in the hall, and if the coat aroused any memories, he did not show it. Certainly he barely glanced at me but, as soon as I appeared, opened the door almost impatiently.

I paused on the steps, entranced by the scene. The amber lights from the house lay across the white lawn and shrouded bushes. It had stopped snowing at last, but the wind continued to shake it from the branches, powdering us lightly. The stars looked like ice particles scattered over the sky.

I said, "Isn't it lovely?"

He made some sound in his throat and took my arm abruptly and helped me down the stairs. I glanced at his face when he got into the car beside me: if this was so distasteful to him, why had he consented to drive me? Amos must have urged him.

Still, he didn't have to take me, even if Amos *had* urged him. Why had he?

Why had he?

Somewhere between the house and the gates the irrational fears began crowding in on me. I told myself I was as bad as Joan, I reasoned with myself. If only he would speak to me, but his face was grim, and his hands seemed to hold the wheel tensely, as if he were under furious control. Accident. . . . Everything that had happened in that house had been an accident.

Did he wonder if I might have seen him after the children had left the pond with Walter; had he been in the thick underbrush, unseen, waiting for us to leave? Did he know I had asked about Julia? I was a stranger, without ties of loyalty to the family. If I suspected her disappearance, would I talk?

He had even given me fair warning. Go home. You may be in danger here.

Had Julia felt in danger from him? Had she left in terror, not even pausing to pack her things? *Had she left at all?*

We climbed slowly to the ridge of the hill from which the children had coasted down on their sleds. The hill dropped down even more sharply on the slope toward town. It was still Freer road and did not become public until it reached the highway. Ernest braked, and the car seemed to waver at the ridge for a long moment before it began its descent.

He said something. I did not catch what it was, but he hunched forward, his hands rigid on the wheels.

Accident. Everything had been an accident.

The car gathered momentum. I had the feeling the wheels were not turning, that we were skimming, sliding. . . . We were out of control. The car slipped headlong. The car would crash, and I would die. An accident. But he would have killed me, and no one would know. We careened. I screamed.

"Let me out!" I reached for the door handle.

"Damn you!" His arm shot across me, pinioning me to the back of the seat.

A wall of snow raced toward us, larger, faster, whiter. It splintered and cracked over us. We were stopped.

I could see nothing but whiteness. We were buried under the snow. I finally caught my breath. My ears rang with the screams I wasn't even conscious of uttering. I turned and looked at him for the first time. He was slumped in the seat, his face shining with sweat.

I dared to say, "What happened?"

"Lucky that snowbank was there," he said, and began to push at the door handle, trying to open his door. He said nothing more, busy with ramming the door hard into the snow over and over again until gradually he managed to open it enough to slip through.

He found a shovel in the trunk and dug the car out as much as he could. I watched him, feeling smaller and smaller and more and more foolish. He came back to the car, started the wipers to clear the snow off the windshield, and turned on the motor. It took almost a half hour to see-saw the car back and forth until he was able to dislodge it and move it out onto the road. We were free; the plowed highway was ahead; we picked up speed going toward Bright River.

I said again, faintly, still ashamed of the way I had acted, "What happened?"

"The road was a sheet of ice. I told Cory to get out with one of the trucks and some sand, but maybe it was too icy for the truck. Or maybe he just forgot."

"I'm sorry I made such a racket," I said. "I was scared to death."

He didn't answer at first, and then he said brusquely, "Are you all right?"

"Just sore, from your arm."

"What were you trying to do, get out at that speed?" His voice was full of contempt.

I said with dignity, "I told you. I was scared."

"So was I," he said. "And with good reason. We could have both been killed."

It would have been another tragic accident. Unbidden, the train of suspicions took off. He had known the road was icy. Is that why he had agreed to drive me to Bright River? But he had told Cory to sand it. Had he told Cory to sand it? If he had crashed the car and I had been killed, wouldn't he have been killed, too? He had just said so himself. We could have both been killed. But did he care about dying? Perhaps it would have been worth it to him to stop my talk, if I talked. His death at any rate would be unclouded by guilt.

Stop, I told myself sharply. I was alive. He had put out his arm to keep me from jumping, maybe to my death. Or, had he stopped me from getting away before I could be killed in the crash?

The village lights were strung out in front of us, as tremulous as the stars. Here were the houses already, like in a Hans Christian Andersen village, cuffed and bearded in snow, icicles hanging heavy from the roofs, chimneys under hoods of snow, porch rails furred with snow, huge drifts towering over the narrow shoveled walks. In spite of my suspicions, my heart lifted with pleasure; I turned and would have shared it with him, except his expression was so forbidding.

He pulled up short in front of the marquee of the Gem Theater and was waiting for me to get out. Halfway out the door I remembered.

"Where and when will I meet you?"

"I'll be at Canuck's. On that corner," he said briefly. "I'll be there when you come out."

I went to the box office and bought my ticket and went inside and found a seat. The feature was already started, and I had not even remembered to see what it was. He might have opened the door for me . . . he might have bought my ticket. . . . No, he was plainly disgusted with me and the way I had acted. He knew I was frightened, he'd told me that before. He knew it was he whom I was afraid of. If he were guiltless—

There were horses and a ranch on the screen, it was a Western, but that was all my whirling brain allowed me to determine. Hot air blew at me from various vents in the ceiling, wafting the odors of buttered popcorn. I felt faintly nauseated. I no longer trusted my own senses. If I had not been infected by the atmosphere of the house, would skidding down an icy hill have seemed to me purposefully evil, directed to hurt me? Had I wronged Ernest? But those holes in the ice, the hatred—

I couldn't breathe that hot popcorn smell. I was dizzy. I stood up, annoying the people past whose knees I had pushed not even a half hour before, and inched my way toward the aisle. Outside, I took great gulps of clean icy air. The streets were still busy with the tag end of Saturday night shoppers. I hesitated. It was too difficult walking and too cold to stay out too long. I stared into drab shopwindows. I thought of having coffee, but the coffee shop was white-tiled and uninviting, I passed the storefront public library, but it was closed. I bought myself a tube of toothpaste in the drugstore, and then there were no more ways to protract the time until I could turn up at the Canuck for my lift home. There was nothing to do but retrace my steps to the bar.

It was crowded with men in mackinaws and earmuffs. A few rawboned young women sat with their young men in the booths against the wall; some stout women stood at the bar with their husbands, drinking beer. The air was filled with smoke, and steam clouded the mirrors, and in the dim lights it took several moments before I found him at the far end of the bar.

A thought that hadn't occurred before paralyzed me: Suppose he is with a girl? But he wasn't. He had seen me now, and so did the two men he was talking to. The three turned, watching me push my way toward them.

I said apologetically, "Am I too early? The picture was terrible."

"We can leave now if you're ready."

The two men had tipped their caps to me and slipped back into the crowd. Ernest put his glass down on the bar.

"Please finish your drink," I said. "I'm in no hurry. As a matter of fact, it's rather fun being out and away from the house for a change."

He remembered his manners. "Would you like a drink?"

"All right. Something mild. With rum."

He waited for my drink and then, carrying both glasses, led me to a booth and slid onto the bench opposite.

I thought feverishly for an opening to conversation, but none came to me. Nor to him, evidently. He looked at his glass as if it displeased him; when he lifted his head, it was to look studiously past me. How can I explain his manner? It was as if he were determined to shut himself away from me, even to refusing to see me.

But the rum finally loosened my tongue. I hadn't

expected to say what I did; the words surprised me almost as much as they did him.

I said, "Why do you dislike me?"

I had shaken him anyway. He took a last gulp of his scotch and put the glass down. "I don't dislike you," he said.

But I was started and not yet ready to lose the impetus. "From the moment I came, from the moment you first saw me that night across the dining-room table, I felt you resented my being there. You didn't even know me, but you resented me. Why?" The words were coming faster and easier now, and I would have gone on except that he lifted his head and looked at me. I stopped.

He said, "Why should it matter to you, how I feel about you?"

Now it was my turn to be disconcerted. "I suppose . . . well, actually it doesn't *matter,* the way you put it. But it *does* matter. We share the same roof; we meet each other now and then. Why does it have to be . . . the way it is? It's uncivilized, pointless anger is. Unless . . . is there a point? If there is, I wish you'd come out with it and let me know."

He had looked away again. He said distantly, "I have nothing against you personally."

Was it that fleeting resemblance to Julia; was that all it was? Or was it only because I was an unknown, a stranger? For an instant it was as if we had touched, but the moment was slipping away, as he was. I held on. "Please tell me. Whatever the reason. You're entitled to dislike me, even unreasonably. But if that's what it is, I'd like to know."

"Are you sure you would?" he said, challenging me.

"Yes."

"I think it was crude of Amos to bring you here."

"Crude?" I caught my breath, bewildered. This was totally unexpected. "I don't know what you mean."

"I think you do."

But he must have realized how genuinely baffled I was. He gave me a hard stare and then dropped his eyes, frowning. "I may have made a mistake," he muttered. "If you don't know—Forget what I said."

"I can't forget it now," I said stubbornly. "I think especially now you owe me an explanation."

"It hasn't to do with you personally," he repeated.

"Then you shouldn't be so reluctant to tell me."

His glance brooded.

"Please," I said. "It would change everything if I understood."

"You asked for it," he said, his mouth hardening. "I thought you were Amos' . . . girl."

My mouth fell open.

"You wanted to know. There it is."

I was still too stunned to feel any anger. That would come later. "But I never saw him before that day he brought me here!"

"So you both said."

"Why should we lie?"

"Come now," he said. "You're not so naïve as all that."

"Why bring me here then? Why not see me where no one would know?"

"He had an adequate reason. As companion for Joan. This way he could watch out for you. Especially now."

Especially now. That meant, the baby.

He amplified. "You're going to have a baby. He didn't

want you to stay alone. When he first broached the idea to us, it seemed a bit contrived, going to New York to find a pregnant girl to be company for his wife. It made more sense if he was looking for an excuse to bring you here."

"I don't see why you call it contrived," I said coldly. "If Joan was frightened to bear her child in this house, where she felt the children were in danger, it seems very reasonable the presence of another woman in her condition might be reassuring."

His glance was ironic. "It seems to me that the very thing that would hurt his wife would be to discover that her husband might have some relation with you other than employer."

The facts were slowly sinking into place. Maybe the very rum that had freed my speech had also fogged my thought processes. I could feel my face grow hot. "Did you think," I began, not really believing it yet, "did you think my baby was Amos'?"

To do him justice he did flinch. "Yes. Isn't it?"

I rose blindly. "I think it's time I went home." The last words were choked.

The people in Canuck's stared at us with interest as we threaded our way through them. As well they might. Here was an employee of the Freer house sharing a booth with Mr. Freer. He was upset, and she looked as if she would break down at any moment. And a baby at least five months on the way. Shrinking within myself, I could almost hear their thoughts.

We got into the car and drove back to Freer's Cove. We made two or three tries on that icy hill before we made it to the top, but this time I was too angry and too humiliated to notice or to care. He left the car at the steps and helped me up into the house.

The hall was dim, lit only by brackets on the walls. I moved past him, but he put out his hand and held me by the arm.

"I'm sorry if you're hurt," he said. "You insisted on knowing. I didn't want to tell you."

I said furiously, "I'd like to say just this: You're not a very good judge of people!"

"I know," he said. "I've been badly taken before." He still held my arm. "Are you a good judge of people?"

Momentarily off guard, I said, "I . . . don't know."

"It would be useful, if you were," he said, and let me go.

It sounded like a warning. Against whom?

4

On Sunday the cold abated and a thick fog rolled in, in the wake of the warmer temperature, but the day was so without light or luster that it hardly seemed like day at all. Maggie grew so restless that Amos offered to haul her on the sleigh for a long ride, and for the hour anyway she was diverted.

Ernest was nowhere to be seen. His car had pulled out of the garage at noon and had not returned. I wondered if his absence had anything to do with me, if he didn't want to confront me again. Whenever I thought of our conversation last night, the indignation would boil up and I'd think of a dozen scathing remarks I could have made. And yet, except for his hurting me with his honesty, his logic was unassailable, the more I thought of it. Coincidence had marked our meeting, without doubt. Ernest's interpretation made no strain on one's credulity. It was far more likely to have happened as Ernest saw it than as it actually was. Ernest needn't reproach himself except for having hurt me, and I saw no reason why that should bother him.

At four o'clock it was almost as dark as night. Matthilde made tea and, in a desperate attempt to amuse the children and relieve the tedium of being with them without interruption, invited me to join them in the nursery. Amos heard her invitation and came along; Joan was immersed in a book, for once. Maggie was delighted to see Amos; he was her favorite ever since he had presented her with Brownie. We stayed there until we looked at each other and laughed: We three adults were all yawning and heavy-eyed. It was a day made for sleep, and Amos excused himself, and then I. I felt guilty for leaving poor Matthilde with the children but there was Mrs. Vinton, I told myself, shutting the door of my room.

For a while I lay across the foot of the bed, leafing through the pages of the month's new magazines, and then I pulled up the folded afghan. Only moments later I gave up struggling and lapsed into sleep.

I don't know how long I slept, only that I wakened to a night sky through the casements and the sound of voices in the hall.

"I don't think so," Amos was saying. "I'll ask Daisy, but I think she's been napping, too."

I was up to open it even before he tapped on the door. Amos' hair looked rumpled from lying on it; he was in moccasins and a sweater.

"Maggie isn't with you, is she? I didn't think she was."

The words had an ominously familiar ring. I looked from Amos to Matthilde's annoyed face. They both seemed calm enough.

"Brownie seems to have got lost," Matthilde said. "Maggie went looking for him, and now I can't find either of them."

"Where's Moira?" I said, my voice unexpectedly sharp.

"Mrs. Vinton is with her. It's Maggie—"

"She's in the house somewhere, so we'll find her," Amos said briskly. "Let's do this systematically. You go through the attic carefully, Matthilde, and Daisy, you take the downstairs. I'll search the cellars, which is where she'll probably be, if I know Brownie."

His briskness calmed me until he stopped me after Matthilde left and said in another voice entirely, "Joan is still asleep. Let's not let her get any wind of this, okay?"

I nodded dumbly and reached for my shoes.

The house is large. The kitchens alone are larger than the entire downstairs of some small houses, and there are hundreds of places where a child and a dog could hide. I went from room to room meticulously, even to the vast cold ballroom where the children never went. I pushed aside each heavy drape and opened each cupboard door and peered behind each stout upholstered chair. Even as I searched, I told myself, she would have revealed herself by now, her span of interest wasn't that long, and the game would have become boring to her already. Besides, she wouldn't be playing this game unless she had already found Brownie, finding him would have been her first concern, and if she had found him, she wouldn't have been able to muffle his delighted yelps.

I was not as fast or as light or as tireless as I once was. I retraced my way, searching as I went, to the main hall. Maybe they've found her already, I thought, standing there, uncertain whether to call down to Amos or up to Matthilde, when the front door opened and Ernest came in.

His clothes were misted with damp, his boots crusted with sand. He followed my glance, and looked down at himself. He said, "I've been sanding that stretch of road. Cory has bronchitis and can't get out of bed."

Is that where you were? Is that what you've been doing?

A change came over him. "What happened?" he said sharply.

"Brownie disappeared, and Maggie went looking for him. We can't find either of them."

He stiffened. He said, "Have you looked through the cellars? I've seen him down there, before."

"Amos is there now."

He made for the cellar door, his sandy boots leaving a trail across the polished floor and the Chinese rugs.

The cellars were as endless as the house, honeycombed with rooms, for the heating plant, the laundry, for wine, for storage, for tools. And each room had a door that could swing shut, too heavy for a four-year-old to open, shutting off her cries. It was taking Amos a long time; maybe that was why Ernest went down, to help him.

Matthilde joined me, her hair disheveled and looking put-out. More than that, guilty. I knew what she was feeling, it was still all too fresh. If she had been alert, Maggie would never have slipped away from her.

"I been over every inch," she said. "I even been to Mr. Freer's room, but Sam said they hadn't seen her."

Maggie would be frantic over her lost Brownie. I was not much older than she when my own dog vanished, and I wandered over Springfield oblivious to time and place until the police caught up with me and returned me to my hysterical mother.

I hesitated beside the cellar door. But they didn't need me. I confess to a hangover from my youth and the days of the Saturday matinee, when in all those haunted houses in all those films a cellar door would creak open above cavernous black depths. I don't like cellars. As I stood trying to prod myself into courage enough to join them below in the search, I felt a draft of cold air. Storm windows and storm doors sealed the house from drafts except when the house was aired in cleaning, and no one cleaned today. A door left open?

I looked around. The cold was coming from the kitchens. I had searched the kitchens before, but now I returned, and saw what I hadn't noticed before. The kitchen door was ajar. And the storm door which enclosed the small entry was open, too. It may have even blown open since I was there last; the latch was off. Or maybe the doors had been left unlatched, but closed, and had been opened by the wind. Who could have unlatched them? They were always closed after the cook had left for the day.

If the doors were ajar, Brownie could have slipped out. If the latches were off, Maggie would have no trouble in following after him.

I didn't stop to think or to tell anyone where I was going. One of the men had left boots and a sheepskin jacket hanging on a hook in the entry hall. I took them; the jacket was large enough to fold over, and my feet were lost in the boots, but I could not wait to go upstairs and find my own outer clothing. Enveloped in the strong smells of leather, sweat, and fertilizer, I went out, closing the door carefully behind me in case Brownie was still by some miracle in the house.

I followed the path to the garage, which was open. Someone had taken a car out hastily. I surveyed the ones still in their places. Amos' car was gone; he must not have found Maggie in the cellar then and had taken the car to search for her on the road.

I made my way to the barn. The lights were on, but there was no one there. At least, no one I could see. It would be the place Brownie might run to; there must be mice among the hay and stacked bags of feed. Where to start—

"What are you doing here?"

I almost fell back. I looked up and saw Ernest leaning down from the balcony rail.

"I thought they might be here," I said, when I recovered my breath.

"I'll take care of these buildings," he said. "You'd better get back to the house."

"I'd like to help."

"You don't have to," he said briefly, and again: "Get back to the house."

He couldn't order me about, I did not work for him. Resistance set in; I squared my chin and started for the doors when he said, "The fog's too thick, and walking is dangerous for you."

Was it actually concern he felt for me? I couldn't believe it. What was the real reason he wanted me back in the house? And yet it did sound almost as if he were concerned.

I paused on the path toward the house.

Still, he had no right to tell me where to go or what to do. I could take care of myself. I stared out past the frozen furrows that marked the truck garden toward the sea.

The cliffs.

I hadn't thought of them before. Maggie had never even ventured near there, but suppose she was trailing Brownie, and he had scampered off in that direction. I barely hesitated, and then I began to plow slowly in my flapping boots across the pristine expanse of snow-covered meadows that led to the sea.

What helped me was the fog's lifting. The wind had strengthened in late afternoon, and now even as I struggled through the snow it had begun to blow the mist away. There was no moon, and in the hazy stretches of sky starting to grow visible there were only stars casting their faint gray light. But it was enough for me to make out the path a man's boots had cut into the snow as I reached the cliffs. Ernest's, no doubt; who else would walk here?

Only as the fog lifted entirely clear of the ground did I see the small prints of a dog. My heart quickened. I was right, and Brownie had been here! The paw prints crisscrossed the plowed track of Ernest's boots, now being lost in it entirely, now appearing on the other side. If Maggie had followed, she would have walked in Ernest's tracks, as I was doing now, to make the going easier.

The snow fence had been dragged down by the weight of the snow, or someone had forced it down, but the track crossed it here to the cliff walk, and I stepped over, still following.

A blur of light behind me made me turn my head; someone had turned on the floodlights that were hung in the eaves of the house. But the light was too far away to reach this part of the cliff walk, and in the darkness I could not make out the paw prints at all. Did they continue? Which way? I had no way of telling if they went on at all. The path was always ragged, worn by the pressure of wind and rain and boots, earth and stone sliding down to the rocks below. The snow had made its edge even more dangerously deceptive. If the path gave way under Brownie, under Maggie . . . they could have both slid down into the sea.

A cold sweat of fear covered me. The pattern of Freer's Cove. The pattern of accident. My mouth was dry, but I tried to raise my voice above the express-train roaring of the wind.

"Maggie! Brownie!"

I crouched on my knees and leaned over as far as I dared. The snow had made a white surface, at least, on which anything that fell would be visible in spite of the darkness.

Nothing. I got back on my feet and plowed on. If they had fallen, they might just as easily have continued their fall on those ice-glazed rocks into the water, leaving no trace. I drove myself on in desperation, though I could hardly lift my feet in their heavy boots to put them down again in Ernest's tracks. Fear had quickened my heartbeat so that the only sound I heard was the pounding of my blood in my ears.

No. Something else. I stopped and strained to hear. It

might have been the wind caught in the rock recesses at the water's edge or the bubbling of the tide trapped there. My stopping may have saved my life.

A crevice cut directly across my path. Even in my fright I saw it was freshly formed, because the boot tracks continued beyond. My legs shook under me. Another step, and my foot would have slipped through, and I would have fallen.

It was while I stood there too shaken to move that I heard the sound again. I strained to listen.

It was the yelping of a dog.

Again I fell to my knees and leaned over the edge. Far below, almost at the water's edge, I saw a dark patch in the snow on a flat, jutting rock. It might have been only where the wind had scoured the snow away. . . . Thin patches of fog still drifted; I blinked, trying to clear my eyes, and leaned over farther.

It almost looked . . . red. The color of Maggie's corduroy overalls.

"Maggie!"

No movement. But again, the faraway yelping of Brownie.

I didn't stop to think or consider my position. If I had, I might have returned to the house for help. I swung my legs over the edge even before I was sure of a foothold or something to cling to. Minutes might count. Half-sitting, half-lying, clutching at any frozen branch or projecting rock, I started the steep slide downward.

I did not dare look below, only to direct myself toward that spot of color that might be Maggie, alive or dead.

"Maggie!"

No answer but Brownie's frantic barking. But the shape

was growing more distinct. It was Maggie. Why didn't she move? Why didn't she make some sign that she heard me?

I was almost at the bottom. The sound of the water was louder, and waves washed over the lower part of the rocks, where patches of ice made them even more perilous. I crawled across the intervening space, I did not dare stand upright.

"Maggie."

I knelt over her. She was on her face. I gently slid my hand under her to turn her around. Now I could see the lacerated skin, the bruises.

"Oh, Maggie darling."

She opened her eyes.

I began to laugh and cry at the same time. I put my arm beneath her and hugged her to me. She screamed with pain.

I noticed then her arm twisted at an odd angle and loose, like the broken wing of a bird.

"I'm sorry, Maggie darling! Lie still!"

I pulled off the sheepskin coat and wrapped her in it as well as I could, trying to push the sides under her so as to protect her from the icy rock. But she cried out in pain when I tried to cover her arm.

"It hurts, Daisy!"

"I know, darling. Lie still. Dr. Raab will fix it as good as new, as soon as we get back."

I was more alarmed by the dull wavering sound of her voice. She must have hurt her head.

"Where is Brownie?"

"He's somewhere around. Can't you hear him?"

"Find Brownie."

I looked around me to see how I could get to where the

yelping was coming from. I still did not dare stand upright. On my hands and knees I dragged myself gingerly across what rocks offered some flat surfaces, now and then feeling the icy water rush up and soak my legs and arms. I scarcely noticed. At last I reached him.

He was tangled in a piece of fisherman's net, wedged into the rocks. How he got there or how he managed to get snared in the netting, I did not stop to speculate about. The netting was stiff with salt, and my fingers were stiff with cold, but I managed finally to free his head and then his paws. Holding him barking and struggling frantically against me, I managed to work my way back to where Maggie lay.

"Naughty dog," she said, in a slurred voice. I put him under the sheepskin beside her. He licked her face, and she cried out, and I had to kneel down beside them both and hold Brownie quiet, but close enough for her to see him.

Now that I was no longer moving I became aware of the water freezing on my arms and legs, of the cold creeping into me, covered only by the wool tunic over my slacks as I was. We had to get up from there as fast as possible, but how? I knew I might not even be able to climb up alone, let alone carrying Maggie.

"I'm going to yell very loudly, Maggie, so someone can hear us and come and get us."

She did not answer, but her eyes watched me.

"Help! Help! Down here, somebody!"

My voice sounded thin and tenuous, borne away by the wind. I tried again, as loud as I could. I stopped for breath and shouted again.

Suppose no one heard us? Would we freeze if we stayed here till morning? Would Maggie survive the night in the cold, with the probable injury to her head and whatever other injury she might have internally? The questions raced through my head while I gathered the strength to shout again.

"Help! Someone help us!"

Maybe we weren't down there the eternity it seemed; each moment seeming to drag on forever. After a while I thought desperately that maybe I should leave her with Brownie and try to get help, but when I said to her, "Maggie, you'll have to stay down here while I go back to the house to get Uncle Amos—" she did not let me finish but rolled her head from side to side.

"Don't go away, Daisy."

There was nothing to do but shout some more.

My voice was hoarse, my throat sore; I had lost all track of time. And then I heard him. Ernest. Unbelievably. From the cliff walk.

"Daisy?"

I tried to swallow, mustering the last shreds of my voice. "We're down here! Maggie's here!"

"Is she all right?"

"She's alive. But hurry."

His descent seemed interminable. I waited, trembling with cold and exhaustion. He reached our rock, and his eyes only skimmed me until they found Maggie. He bent over her without a word, but his face looked angry. Only then did he turn to look at me.

"I'll carry her up first and then come back for you."

"I can manage myself," I said, my teeth chattering.

"Don't try it," he said briefly. "I'll be back." He reached down and scooped up Maggie in his arms. She made no sound, though he had to move her broken arm, so I knew she must have slipped into unconsciousness. Better that way.

"Put your coat around you," he said.

"Maggie—"

"I'll cover her with my coat."

I kept Brownie with me. I heard the scrabbling of Ernest's boots on the rocks, and I thought, he'll fall with Maggie, and we'll all die here, and then I did not dare look but huddled on the rock with Brownie buttoned in my coat with me. Ernest was standing over me, wearing only a sweater now.

"Okay, let's go."

"Is she all right alone?"

"She's rolled up in my coat, well away from the path. I'll take Brownie."

I transferred the puppy to him and got shakily to my feet.

"You go first," he said. "I'll be behind you, backing you up."

There were times when he pulled and pushed, times when he went ahead of me so that I could grasp his hands, times when he half carried me. The mind has a capacity to blot out the stress of its worst moments; all I remember is that when I thought I could go no farther his hands pushed me up onto the path.

I walked ahead of him toward the house, again carrying Brownie so he would not run away, Ernest following with Maggie. The walking was good for me; it restored the circulation in my legs; I was even able to breathe more calmly. Could I have hurt my baby? Dr. Raab had said I was strong, as strong as those proverbial pioneer women who had their babies in the fields. That strength had certainly been put to the test tonight.

As we neared the house, headlights cut a path in front of the garage. The car stopped, and Amos got out; for a moment he seemed to peer at us, as if not certain that it was truly us, and then he ran toward us.

"You have Maggie. Thank God. What happened? Where did you find her?"

Even Ernest was too exhausted for explanations. "She fell from the cliff, going after Brownie. Daisy found her. Let's get her to Raab as fast as possible."

"I'll drive," Amos said. "You get in the back seat with Maggie."

He seemed to notice me for the first time. "Daisy, are you all right?"

"I think so."

"Maybe you ought to come with us and let Raab have a look at you too."

I shook my head. "I'm too cold. If I think I need him, I'll call him. Right now all I want to do is get warm."

I shed the boots and jacket in the kitchen entry and made my way with an effort to our apartment.

"Daisy?" Dear Lord, Joan.

Her voice was taut with alarm. I had to drag my weary frozen self to her room.

"What happened? Look at you! What happened?"

Had she spoken to Amos? How much did she know? My mind was too tired to function smoothly. "Everything is all right—"

"I want to know what happened," she said sharply.

I said, "Brownie ran out of the house, and Maggie chased

him to the cliffs. They both fell. I found them, and Ernest found me, and Amos and Ernest are taking her to Raab to set her arm. But she's going to be fine."

She sank back against the pillows, her eyes piercing me as if I had withheld something. "You're telling me the truth, Daisy?"

"The whole truth," I said tiredly. "Now, will you let me go and get into a warm bath?"

She gasped, "I *am* sorry. Poor Daisy. I'll phone Mrs. Vinton to come and help you."

I stripped my cold wet clothes off in the bathroom, and without waiting for the tub to fill up I got in and let the hot rushing water bring some feeling back into my frozen feet. By the time the water reached my neck I was feeling better. Mrs. Vinton rapped on the door and came in to help me up, enfolding me in a huge bath towel and briskly rubbing my arms and back.

"Matthilde and I were half out of our minds. That lump of a girl must have gone to sleep when she should have been watching Maggie. I kept thinking: Oh, Lord, let it not be another one," said Mrs. Vinton, helping me into bed, pushing a hot-water bag under my feet.

She brought me hot tea. By now I was flushed all over and as pink as a strawberry and feeling deliciously languid. I must have dozed with my lamp still on, and when I opened my eyes, it was to see Amos standing at the foot of the bed.

"Sure you're not on fire?" he said, putting his cold fingers to my blazing cheeks. "I brought you some brandy."

"Don't need any, thanks," I said drowsily. "How's Maggie?"

"She has a concussion. Raab set her arm and thought she'd

better spend the next day or two in the hospital. Other than some bad scratches and bruises she's all right. When you think what might have happened to her—" He stopped. He looked more haggard than he had any right to, considering the outcome. He said, "All I could think was, and I had to be the one to give her that damned puppy."

"But it was an accident!"

Our eyes met. Again.

"Of course it was. I know that. Ernest said the ground must have given way under the snow. But—"

But one's credulity was sorely tested. The fourth accident, two of them fatal, two near misses.

"If you hadn't found her," he said, "she would probably have died from exposure. If she hadn't already been dead from the fall."

"Someone else would have found her before the night was over. Brownie was barking. That's how I knew where she was."

Hazily my mind remembered troubling details. The latches unbarred—Only the cook had come from Bright River that day, and it wasn't like her to be careless. Still, Cory might have come in. No, he was in his bed with bronchitis. Amos or Ernest, on their way outside? But the latches must have been left open before then, to enable Brownie to get out.

And the fishnet. How had he become entangled in the fishnet? It must have been washed up on the rocks, and he had fallen on it, and somehow ensnared himself. Why had he gone to the cliffs in the first place?

I murmured it out loud.

"I wonder," said Amos. "Still, I bought him from Ed

Jagger, whose house is on the water. Maybe Brownie remembered the smell of salt water, maybe he got a whiff of it through the open door and went after it—"

My eyes were closing.

"Get some sleep," he said, bending over me and kissing my cheek. "I came in to say thanks, but how can I say it? On behalf of all of us, thanks, Daisy. Thanks for saving Maggie's life."

I heard him leave. I heard the knock on the outer door and heard Amos open it. I heard Ernest's voice.

"How's Daisy?"

"She's fine. She's sleeping."

That was all I heard. I fell asleep thinking: He asked after me. He actually took the trouble to come up to ask after me. Ernest. In my sleep I remembered the touch of his arms helping me, holding me.

4

It was decided among all of us that Frances and Walter not be told of the accident. Maggie was in no danger, and they would be home in a few days anyway. Amos went to meet them when they stepped out of the plane at Portland and broke the story gently to them on the drive to Freer's Cove. When they entered the house, looking tanned and healthy, they were prepared to scold Maggie for her rash behavior.

Maggie's arm was still in a cast, so the scolding was a minimum and the embraces tender. "This child!" cried Frances. "Imagine her having the audacity to go out in that deep fog to the cliffs! I'm afraid she's going to take after me!" There was ill-concealed pride in her voice.

"And endurance, too," I said. "She had only a light sweater on over her overalls."

She turned to me. "You risked your life and your baby's for her sake, Daisy. How will I ever be able to thank you enough?"

Her gratitude embarrassed me. I was even more embarrassed a week later when a package arrived for me from a New York jeweler, containing a heavy and handsome gold bangle. The card in it said: "This is only an infinitesimal token of how much we owe you."

I felt I had been forgiven for what part I had been blamed for in the death of Jeffrey.

It appeared the episode was over, but I hadn't reckoned on the long memory of Frances; she seemed to have the same tenacity she had once attributed to her brother Amos.

Amos and Joan had gone to New York on their delayed visit to the doctor, Maggie's heavy cast was reduced to a light one and a sling, and Frances invited me in to her rooms for afternoon tea. She began without preliminary, so I knew this was the purpose of her invitation.

"How did Maggie manage to get away from Matthilde that afternoon?"

I was unprepared. I began, "Why . . . I suppose—"

"Matthilde would never have let her out of her sight if she'd been awake."

I thought back to that afternoon, trying to reconstruct it. Actually the drama of finding Maggie had wiped from my mind any thought of what had preceded it, beyond the actual details of how she and Brownie had managed to get out of the house. This continued to trouble me from time to time when I thought of it, and now and again when I remembered I would pass the kitchen entry and look to see if it was closed. It always was, unless the cook was more attentive than usual after what had happened. But earlier. . . .

"We left Maggie with Matthilde in the nursery. Brownie was there. Matthilde had invited Amos and myself in to tea—"

"You drank tea," she said slowly. "And then what?"

"Well . . ." I floundered. "It was one of those days, Frances. A gray heavy fog, and we were cooped up in the house all day. I remember we all were getting drowsy. Even Amos kept yawning and finally went back to his room for a nap. I slept, too. I hated to leave Matthilde; it must have been an effort for her to chase around after Maggie when it would have been such a delicious afternoon for sleep." I stopped. I remembered Matthilde's rather vacuous face yawning and yawning, her eyes reddening with tears as she blinked them open.

Frances was watching me, her mouth thinned to a line.

"So she could have gone to sleep after you left."

"She wouldn't have left the children," I said.

"No, she could have fallen asleep in her chair long enough for Maggie to get away after Brownie."

"It is possible, Frances—"

"And you all drank tea."

"Frances, you know what it's like by four in the afternoon, if there's nothing to do, and the house is warm and stuffy, and—"

"Yes, you might have felt drowsy. But Matthilde does not fall asleep in the afternoons. I have never seen her asleep, even though she's lethargic by temperament, not at all like Amy."

"You weren't here. I suppose servants do relax when their employers are away."

"Daisy, *where was Ernest?*"

"Come now, Frances! You're not suggesting he was hovering invisible around the teapot, are you?"

"I am suggesting that when Matthilde was in the nursery he could have gone into the kitchen and put some sleeping pills in the teapot."

"How would he know she would make tea?"

"You know the habits of this family by now. We generally have tea at this time. The children always have a snack, milk or cocoa, and when I'm home, I invariably join them. Matthilde has something with them, just as Amy used to." She paused. "Ernest has lived in this house long enough to be aware of our habits."

"Ernest was outside that Sunday sanding the hill with the dump truck. Cory was sick in bed, and there was no one else around to do it. I saw him when he came in."

"When was that? Before Maggie disappeared, or after?"

I said slowly, "After, I guess."

"You were asleep when Jeffrey died," she said quietly. "And Amy was asleep when Ronnie drowned."

She did not have to point out to me the deadly pattern.

"I'll tell you this much," she said grimly. "We are going to see that the children are never left unguarded for a moment from now on. I've told Walter to engage a man, and though we'll give him odd jobs to do around the house, his real purpose will be to watch those children night and day."

In a few days Hollis joined the household. He wore a

houseman's jacket, and I saw him clean windows and polish
silver, but wherever Matthilde was with the children, Hollis
was invariably within sight.

I think everyone felt as if a great burden had been light-
ened when Hollis came. I know I did, and the change was
noticeable in Joan. She was even eager to talk of the past.
She talked of how she met Amos, and of their honeymoon in
Italy, and of how she wanted to go back. I sighed when she
talked. Jed and I had spent a fast weekend in a motel in
Westhampton before we returned to that dingy room.

"Next time it's going to be different, Daisy," she said.
"When you meet someone you'll love, who'll love you. It has
to happen to you. It's time good things begin to happen for
you."

She could talk freely enough about my future, but never
her own, just as she would question me about my symptoms
but never mention her own. She wanted to know when the
baby moved inside me and what it felt like. "Is it the same
with you?" She would nod, but volunteer nothing further. I
wondered if she had a kind of primitive fear of talking or
thinking about her child, as if she might chance the envy
of the gods.

And why wasn't she making plans for the baby's coming?
People made lists and left orders in department stores, even
if nothing was to be delivered till the day of birth. It was as
if she didn't believe her baby would actually be born or that
she did not dare express it openly, again, so as not to chal-
lenge fate.

I had made a small list for my baby. Although I hadn't
been in touch again with the adoption agency, I knew that

181

its custom was to take over the child as soon as it was born, if possible. Even so, I would have to travel with him to New York to surrender him to them, and he would need some clothing. I made myself face this fact, of giving him up as soon as possible. It would be best for me as well as for him; we would not have the chance to grow accustomed to each other. The longer we were together, the harder it would be to separate myself from him.

I kept urging her to order what she would need, and finally, when there was a change in the air, a new color to the light, a soft humidness to the salty wind, all of which meant spring, she said, "All right, Daisy. Maybe it would be a good idea if you and Frances drove into Boston. She's experienced, she'll know what to buy better than I could tell you."

Frances was glad to get away, now that Hollis was here. We left early Saturday morning and were in Boston before noon. We picked out a crib and a large handsome carriage, stacks of microscopic underthings and outer things, blankets, sweaters, linens, diapers. All would be delivered on the day we called for them. I brought back with me a small parcel of what I thought I would need for my own child, plus a small bonnet and a yellow rubber duck, because they were irresistible. And then on impulse I bought a second bonnet, and a second rubber duck, as a gift for Joan. I thought they might make her baby more of an actuality to her.

"Ridiculous," grumbled Frances on the drive home. "Spending a fortune on furniture when her baby could have Moira's."

"A first baby is special. I think everything should be new."

Frances said evenly, "Maybe Joan thinks my children's things have a curse on them."

Maybe.

As soon as we came home, I ran upstairs with the tiny ribboned hat and the yellow rubber duck, but Joan only smiled at them, and let them lie on top of her quilt. I packed what I had bought for my baby in the special small overnight bag I would take with me to the hospital. It was large enough for his few things, and I packed them with dispatch, not allowing myself to dwell on them too long. Still, they were as fine as I could buy, as fine as what I had bought for Joan. I would send him out into his new world at least handsomely dressed, since that would be all I would be able to do for him.

I was not to be allowed to forget what had happened yet.

On my next visit to Dr. Raab, Maggie came along to have the last of her cast removed. Frances drove us. As always, Brownie went with Maggie. When we went into the waiting room Maggie looped his leash around the back of her chair.

I was called first, then Maggie.

"You watch him, Daisy," she told me solemnly.

"I will."

"If someone whistles, don't let him get away the way he did that night."

Frances and I exchanged glances. What was on our minds had to wait until they had emerged again, Maggie's arm looking skinny and white but whole, free of its cast at last. We got into the car, and almost at once Frances said, casually, "Who whistled for Brownie that night he ran away?"

Maggie shrugged indifferently.

Her mother persisted. "Did you see who whistled?"

Maggie shrugged, shook her head.

"Then how do you know someone whistled?" Frances said impatiently.

"I heard it, Mommy. It was outside the door."

"Did you go to see who it was?"

She shook her head. "I didn't know it was for Brownie. And then when I looked for him, he wasn't there."

"Did you run after him right away?"

"Unh-unh." She shook her head. "I waked up Mattie, but she wouldn't wake up."

Again I met Frances' eyes.

"What do you mean, she wouldn't wake up?" said Frances sharply. "Did you shake her?"

Maggie nodded. "And I asked her to come with me to find Brownie, but she just snored. And I pulled her hand, but she didn't wake up."

"How did you know where Brownie went?"

"He was *barking*," she said, as if we were stupid not to know that. "I heard him barking downstairs, and I went downstairs. And then I heard him barking in the kitchen, and he wasn't in the kitchen, but I heard him barking outside going to the barn, only he wasn't in the barn, and I heard him running to the ocean, Mommy, and I was afraid he would fall in. And he did."

We were silent.

I said at last, "Did you see Brownie going to the cliffs?"

"It was almost *nighttime*," she said, scornful of my stupidity to ask. "And foggy. I couldn't see *anything*."

"How did you know where he was then?" asked Frances.

"He was still barking, Mommy."

"How did you fall down, Maggie?" I said carefully.

"I was looking for him. I heard him, but I couldn't see him. And then there was a great big hole, and I stepped in it, and I fell and I got hurt."

"I know, darling. I know," said Frances.

She left the car for Hollis to park, and sent Maggie up to Matthilde, but lingered to talk to me.

"Matthilde denies being asleep, but of course she would. I believe Maggie."

I believed her, too. She was too straightforward a child, and not particularly imaginative.

"Who could have whistled for Brownie?"

"Sam, maybe?"

"Sam never leaves my father. And why would he want to take the dog from Maggie?"

She looked at me.

I could not answer.

She expressed my unspoken thought: "And you and Amos were both drugged with the same tea."

Which left Ernest. Again.

"Frances, I know what's in your mind. But Ernest *saved* us. I don't know how long Maggie would have survived if he hadn't come and helped us both up the cliff."

"He found her after you found her. When he knew she would survive anyway. Oh, I don't think of him as a cold-blooded killer, Daisy. He is my own brother. But I think a cloud of depression settles over him, when he is not accountable for what he does. And maybe when it lifts, he doesn't even remember, or if he does remember, he is so overwhelmed with guilt that he can't speak to us or even look at us."

Her voice fell away.

"Here is something I've never told anyone, not even my husband. Where is Julia? That woman would never have gone away of her own accord and left a sable coat behind, and most of her jewels. I know her. Where is she, Daisy? What did Ernest do to her?"

I managed to find my voice, though I was more shaken than I had a right to be. Who was Ernest to me, after all, that her story should sicken me as it did? "Can't you arrange for a psychiatric examination if you think he's that ill?" I said faintly.

She said, "I'm afraid for my father. If he even suspected Ernest of such dreadful things, it would kill him. Besides dragging our name into the mud. Can you imagine the scandal? No, I have safeguarded my children, at least. The rest will have to wait until—"

But she could not finish the sentence, as if even the thought of her father's death was too much to contemplate. I went up to my room, still feeling sick at heart. Perhaps it was only pity, perhaps gratitude for his saving our lives that night. But maybe it was more. I realized for the first time that I did not want Ernest to be a murderer. The realization confounded me.

V

I HAD MONTHS TO PREPARE for the end of my stay at Freer's Cove, but when the time came, it was abrupt, and bewilderingly, too soon.

There was a drift of crocuses under the elms and maples on the lawn, pushing up through the patches of snow. The willows were yellow, casting a haze of yellow pollen on the softening ruts of earth beneath them, and Dr. Raab said to me on my last visit, "A week maybe. Keep your bag packed."

Joan and Amos left for New York, for what might be their last visit before their baby came. Dr. Raab had engaged a room for me in the hospital in Portland, and Frances or Walter would drive me there when the time came, should Amos not have returned. They had said no word to me yet about my leaving: I wondered. We had grown so close these past months that it seemed to me that they must feel as reluctant as I to terminate our relationship, and I thought they might suggest that I stay, at least for the summer any-

187

way, until it was time for me to go back to school. Unless they thought it might be too painful for me to see them with their baby when I no longer had my own. Unless Amos thought I would only serve to remind Joan of a distressing period in their lives.

I speculated, and I thought about the baby and giving it up, and I thought about Freer's Cove and how though it was a tragic place, still I did not want to leave it. And I thought of Ernest.

More and more his lonely figure setting off on his nightly walks to the cliffs preoccupied my mind. I found myself watching him from my window in the lengthening days when I could see him more clearly, his head a little bent, his brown hair ruffled by the wind, his hands in the pockets of his mackinaw, striding across the lawns. Did he walk like a murderer? What was in his mind as he walked?

I wished I could walk with him; I thought if I ever could talk easily to him, without the constraints of fear and suspicion on my side and distrust on his, I would be able to tell soon enough what kind of man he was. With Joan and Amos gone I had more time on my hands, more time to think, but I did not have the courage to go after him.

We expected Amos and Joan home from New York on Sunday night. Instead there was a telephone call for me.

It was Amos.

"Daisy, the doctor says Joan's time is so close now it might be more sensible for us to stay on in New York."

I was as excited as if it were my own baby so imminent. "When? Did the doctor say?"

"He wasn't sure, but he thought it best to take no more

chances. Our hotel is only minutes away from the hospital, and from his office, too."

I only then wondered at the tenseness of his voice. Was it just excitement? "But does the doctor seem pleased with her? Is it going all right?"

"Well . . ."

"Tell me, Amos."

"It's still touch and go. But there *is* something. It's selfish of us to ask you, with the ordeal ahead of you."

"Please ask me. Anything."

"Daisy, I know Joan would be a lot easier if you were with her."

Unexpectedly, my heart sank. I said, "I'll be only too happy to come, only"—I took a breath—"only I'm not sure what day I'll be going to the hospital myself. Dr. Raab said one day this week."

"I wouldn't have asked you, Daisy, if I hadn't called Raab first. I wouldn't have you volunteering to do anything that could be dangerous. But he anticipated no problem. He said anyone in New York could deliver the baby, if it should come while you were there."

"Then of course I'll come," I said. "Are you at the Lanning again?"

"Yes. If you tell me when you'll be here, I'll engage a room for you."

"I'd better come as soon as possible. I'll be on the first plane out in the morning."

"Daisy, you're wonderful. I can't tell you how much I appreciate it."

"I'll have to find out about the planes."

"Wire me from the airport when you leave, and I'll be waiting for you at LaGuardia."

But he didn't hang up at once. It was almost as if he sensed some reservation in me. "You're sure you don't mind?"

"Sure, Amos." And I was truly glad I could help her. Only . . . I didn't understand. Maybe it was that I was leaving Freer's Cove so suddenly. I had the feeling of things beginning . . . left undone. And yet, what? The mystery of the children? Was it a mystery? Ernest? Even he was no longer mysterious, only an unhappy man brutally robbed of his daughter. Julia? Here I faltered. No. What were the Freers to me? Once I left this house I would never see any of them again. I said hesitantly, "It's just that Dr. Raab—I mean, he's my doctor, and . . . I guess I'm used to him."

"In some ways it will be simpler like this, Daisy. You'll have your baby in New York. The agency is in New York. They can come and take him there."

His words chilled me. I don't know why. He was only telling me what I knew, what I had told him to begin with. Perhaps it was too close now, and I was being forced to face the future.

We said good-bye, and I sent my love to Joan. He added almost offhandedly, "Tell Frances and Walter. Tell them that when we come back, there'll be three of us, I hope."

I promised I would, I wished them luck again, and I hung up the receiver and went across the hall to tell Frances.

"I'll be glad when it's over," she said. "I wonder how it will turn out."

"For the best, we hope," said Walter heartily. "But what's this, Daisy? You're leaving us? For good?"

Frances had been so absorbed in the news about the baby that she had hardly heard about my leaving. Now her face fell, and I actually think she was sorry. "You've become part of our lives, Daisy. Even if you hadn't saved Maggie's life, you've grown dear to us. If I didn't know it was more important for you to go on with your education and your career, I'd ask you to stay on. We'd find something for you to do here."

Pride would not have allowed me to stay if Amos and Joan did not want me.

"It's back to work for me," I said, trying to smile and failing. "I told Amos I'd catch the morning plane."

"That leaves around eleven," Walter said, rising. "Let me call the airport in Portland and check."

He called, and reserved a seat for me on the eleven ten. I marveled at how quickly and easily I was slipping away from Freer's Cove, almost as suddenly as I'd become a part of it.

"We'll get you to the airport, Walter or I," Frances said. "And if by any chance we're tied up with Father or the children, Hollis will take you."

I was practically on my way already. "I'd better start packing," I said.

"In any case, we'll see you before you leave," Frances said.

I went to my room and dragged out my father's valise and opened it on the bed. I didn't want to leave. I knew that, but I wasn't yet ready to face the reason. As I folded the contents of the bureau drawers back into the valise, I could only remember the night I had come, and the strangeness, and how I'd even thought of not undressing, as if my clothes would serve as protection against this large, somber house. How frightening the maze had seemed, where a child had died, where another might have died. A cursed place. Now I hadn't even thought of the maze in weeks. I went to the window to look down on it, as if to see if it still evoked any emotion.

There was still some twilight left. Even as I looked down from my window, I could see Ernest standing motionless in the maze, beside the wishing well. I could see only a part of his face above the short beard; the rest was hidden by the yews, but there was something overwhelmingly sad in the way he stood there. It pierced me. I had an impulse to weep for him. Even as I watched, he moved away, threading his way though the maze. Night descended with a low bank of purple-backed clouds. I could barely make out his form moving inevitably toward the cliffs.

I would not see him before I left. Tomorrow was Monday, and he would be gone for Bright River before I was up. I could wait for his return and say good-bye to him then, or I could walk out toward the cliffs and meet him there. I felt somehow there would be less constraint if we met outdoors, in the darkness. Here with the chance of Frances or Walter coming down and interrupting us, in the lamplight where he could see me clearly and I could see his face with his eyes that could be so unfriendly and his expression so utterly without warmth, I would not be able to say the words I wanted to say.

And what were they? I could not tell him that I did not think him capable of killing his wife, let alone a child. I could imagine his eyes narrowing as if I had gone completely mad. I could only say that I was sorry there had been so little time for us to know each other, that I'd never properly thanked him for that night when he'd saved us, that I was . . . sorry for him . . . and hoped that he be happier someday. Probably my courage would fail me before I could say anything, but certainly I would feel braver in the dark.

I hesitated. I don't know how long it was before I finally put on my red coat and boots and let myself out of the apartment. When I went downstairs, I noticed with surprise that a strange car stood outside the main doors. Maybe Frances or Walter had a visitor. I made my way to the back of the hall and let myself out through the patio.

When I passed the maze, it was with hardly a sidelong look; resolutely I headed toward the ocean. My boots sank into the spongy soil, and there was a strong fresh smell of earth that I hadn't been aware of since October. The night air was scaldingly fresh and blowing hard from the water, sweeping my hair straight back from my face. It had been months since I'd walked at night, and I was full of the sense of guilty pleasure, for behaving rashly and incautiously. Would I really say any of the things I planned to say, or would I lose heart and pretend that the meeting was an accident?

I reached the cliffs. Carefully I stepped over the trodden-down section of snow fence and from here on began to walk more gingerly, clinging to the line of red fencing as much as possible. There was no sign of Ernest, though I had been sure I'd be meeting him at once on his way back to the house. Could I have missed him, delaying so long in making up my mind that he had already returned without my seeing him? And then I heard his voice.

It was still some distance beyond, and though the night

was clear with the light of half a moon, I could still not see that far ahead. I heard his voice low and urgent. It gave me an eerie feeling; he seemed to be talking to himself, and all those thoughts of his illness came back to me, and my skin prickled. But even as I stood there, uneasily, I heard another voice, a woman's. It seemed to start low and then mount higher, strangely piercing, and then I knew it was laughter I heard. I was transfixed. That high piercing laughter sounded over the wind and the water, sharp as a knife.

Suddenly there were running steps. The steps were coming closer, funneling down the narrow path toward me. I stepped back, but I could not outrun them. I pressed into the snow fence, holding on with both hands even as it bent beneath me, staring at the figure in terror. It reached me; it stopped.

It was a woman's shape, real or illusory I still was not sure. Black hair thick on her shoulders, tall, wrapped in furs. Her voice said, "Who the hell are you?" and then she ran on, her laughter lower now, laughter full of fury.

She was real. I think I knew at once who she was. I was still faint with that first panic, and I stood there until Ernest came toward me.

"What are you doing out here?"

But his voice held none of the other hostility. It sounded tired.

"I came out . . . for a walk."

"Did you?" He gave a short laugh. "You picked a fine night for it. You had the rare chance to meet my wife."

So it *was* Julia. And she was alive.

"Why was she here?" I said huskily.

"To get some jewelry and her fur coat. And to tell me she was flying to Mexico for a divorce if I agreed."

Julia. Alive.

"I told her she couldn't have a damn thing except the divorce." His voice roughened. "She was welcome to it. She said it was too bad I felt that way, but she'd taken the precaution of taking the jewelry out of the safe before she met me. She couldn't find the coat." Again that short laugh.

He seemed suddenly to become aware of me.

"You shouldn't be walking here at night. It's slippery underfoot. Get on the other side of the fence."

He stepped on it to hold it down and helped me over it. He took my arm. The touch of his hand on my arm seemed to dry up the words I had intended to say. The house loomed ahead; soon there would be no more time. I stopped and looked up at him.

"Actually, I came out to find you. I wanted to say goodbye."

"Good-bye?" He sounded taken aback.

I explained about my sudden leaving for New York. "I suppose I won't be seeing you or Freer's Cove again," I said. "I did want to tell you that . . . in spite of . . . a misunderstanding I—I mean, dreadful things happened here, and we were all involved, but—" I didn't know how to go on. "I love it here," I stammered. "I'll miss it."

"You're different from my wife," he said. "She just told me how glad she was to be out of it, how she hoped never to see Freer's Cove or me again."

He stared down at me.

"It's hard to believe," he said. "So you will really miss it?"

"I will miss . . . all of you. Everything."

He took my arm again, and we walked toward the house. His head was bent, and his forehead wrinkled, and he seemed profoundly disturbed. It must be the meeting with Julia that had shaken him, I thought; certainly it could have nothing to do with me or my going away.

But when we reached the patio doors, and he held them open for me to go through, he said, still holding my arm, "I knew you would be leaving one of these days. Still, I didn't realize it would be . . . so soon."

And then his glance went past me into the house, and his face changed. He dropped my arm abruptly and went out the way we had come. Bewildered, I followed the direction of his glance. Julia stood there, leaning against the door, her huge eyes rimmed with mascara and weighted down with false eyelashes watching me mockingly. In her arms she carried a sumptuous sable coat.

She half smiled when I noticed it.

"I'm not stealing it," she said. "It's mine. I knocked on Frances' door and told her to give it to me. I knew she'd have it stashed away somewhere when I couldn't find it in my closet. I told her Ernest said for me to have it, and she didn't dare not give it to me."

Her triumphant glance swept over me; her eyes narrowed. "But that's my old coat you're wearing!"

"Frances didn't think you'd want it anymore," I said. "Would you like it back?"

She laughed. "Keep it. I have everything I want from this house and this family. Everything." She patted her large handbag meaningfully. I suppose she had put the jewelry in it.

196 ❧

She said, "Whose baby are you carrying? Is it a Freer? But it must be born in wedlock to inherit; didn't Frances tell you?"

I didn't bother to answer. In spite of her laughter and her bold composure I sensed it was hysteria I heard in her voice, and there was no point in allowing myself to be offended.

"I thought you two were rather cozy as you came in. So that's why Ernest is allowing me to divorce him! I wondered. He sang another tune the other times when I begged him for it."

Her mouth worked. She flung open the front door. Now I could see a man sitting at the wheel of the car. As Frances had surmised, there had been someone waiting to take care of her, and more than adequately, if the long gleaming car was an indication.

"At least, he still likes my type," she said, and ran out and down the steps and into the car. The car hummed expensively down the drive.

I shut the door and went up the stairs to my room. I went quietly, so that Frances wouldn't hear and intercept me. I did not feel up to comparing notes on Julia and her performance here tonight. The only fact that drummed in my brain was: Julia is alive. Ernest did not murder her.

I stared at my strapped suitcase and the overnight bag that would go with me to the hospital. Depression returned, a weight in my chest, a thickness in my throat.

What a damn fool I had been.

Julia's return alive and unharmed threw everything that had happened in this house into an entirely different perspective. Although I gave lip service to the theory of accidents I had actually succumbed to the atmosphere of Freer's

Cove; with all my brave talk and assured pose I had allowed myself to be infected by Frances' suspicions and Joan's fears. Now I knew what a fool I was and how much I had wasted on my own fears and suspicions. What a damn, silly fool!

I laughed at myself, and I cried, out of the depths of the despondency that had engulfed me, and because I had nothing better to do, I went into the kitchen and put up the kettle for tea.

There was a knock on my door.

Not Frances, not tonight.

I went to open it. Ernest stood there.

I must look a fright. Could he tell I'd been crying? He still looked too deeply disturbed to notice.

He said, "How are you leaving tomorrow?"

"On the eleven ten plane from Portland," I said. "Hollis is taking me to the airport."

"I'll drive you," he said.

"Really you don't have to bother. It's Monday, and you'll be going to the plant—"

"It's no bother," he said, standing there.

Silence. I said uncertainly, "Will you have some tea? I'm making some for myself."

"Thanks."

He came in awkwardly, and I went back to the kitchen for the tea things. He waited at the door and took the tray from my hands and brought it to the table in front of the sofa. He frowned at the teacup I gave him, as if it were the source of his preoccupation, and I searched feverishly for a way to break through to him.

I said, "You must be very upset. It's shocking when someone you loved asks to end a marriage."

"It hardly touches me now," he said. "It might have once, but that was years ago."

At least he was talking to me. He still stared absorbedly at the cup in his hand.

"She makes Ronnie fresh in my mind, that's all. Ronnie was very much like her," he said. "That will hurt for a long time."

I saw suddenly that he wanted to talk, and I sipped my tea and waited.

"It never was much of a marriage," he said. "Julia's beautiful, and I was in love with her. But that was all, there was nothing on her side for me. I could take her out of her father's house on Wharf Street; I could pay her bills at resort hotels where she met the kind of men she preferred. When I knew, my pride was hurt, and I struck out at her, and our life here was hell, even before Ronnie died. I knew there was a man waiting for her. She told me. She preened herself over him, because he could give her more than I could. But by that time nothing she did really touched me anymore."

"You knew she ran away from you?" I said faintly. "You knew, and yet you— Why didn't you say?"

But how could he know what Frances thought, what I thought?

He said, "It was a question of pride. I couldn't give Frances the satisfaction of knowing she was right. She guessed it would end the way it did."

"Everything seems so simple, suddenly, so . . . almost commonplace. When I first came here, it seemed as if a dark pall hung over everyone, it was an unhappy house—"

He said quietly, "It *is* an unhappy house."

"But—"

"You're best out of it," he said. "There's hate here, and . . . sickness. Go back to New York and have your baby and forget you ever knew us."

I stared at him, bewildered.

He stood up. "You better get some sleep," he said abruptly. "We'll have to leave at nine to make the plane comfortably."

I stared after him, and the depression settled over me again. He had shaken me and darkened the air.

I was ready before nine. Sam came in to take my bags down and I asked him, "Is Mr. Freer awake? I'd like to say good-bye."

"Sure, you go in," he said.

Mr. Freer was still in bed, propped up on hemstitched linen pillow cases against the carved back of his walnut bed. He stared at me dully, as if he were not sure who I was.

"I'm going back to New York, Mr. Freer. I wanted to say good-bye and to thank you for being so nice to me."

His lips trembled. "Why don't you stay?"

"I'm going to have my baby."

He nodded. Two tears appeared, in the corner of each eye. "Ronnie died. And Jeffrey. Two of my grandchildren are dead."

"I know. It was dreadful." His speech was mumbling, and not all the proper sounds were made, but I had learned to distinguish his words by now. I gave him my hand and pressed his. "I must go now. Ernest is taking me to the airport."

He did not let my hand go. "Careful. You must be careful."

"I will be. Amos will be meeting me in New York and taking me to their hotel."

His large gaunt head, a travesty of what must have been once a striking one, shook.

"Careful. Careful."

"I will be. Good-bye, Mr. Freer."

"Sick," he said, his head shaking. "Sick man."

"You'll be better soon," I said, managing to draw my hand away. His eyes stared after me as I left, his head shaking.

A small procession accompanied me down to the front door, Frances, carrying Moira, Maggie and Brownie, Walter, and then Matthilde and Mrs. Vinton. I kissed them all; they kissed me.

Ernest was waiting outside at the car. He helped me in.

"You'll bring the baby back and let us see him!" cried Frances.

I nodded and waved, and fastened my seat belt.

"Good-bye! Good-bye!" they called and waved as we rolled down the drive. My throat was full. I blinked. I wanted to see the house for the last time, the long driveway bordered with rhododendron, the leaves that had been pinched and folded all winter with cold now wide and glossy, the tall iron gates that had loomed before my dazzled eyes the first night Amos had brought me here opening for the last time to usher me out.

Cory was there, cap in hand.

"Good-bye, Mrs. Holland!"

"Good-bye, Cory!"

We climbed the hill where the children sledded and coasted down the steep side where I'd been sure I was meant to die, and now we were on the turnpike and going fast, and Freer's Cove was lost in the pine forests. I found my handkerchief and blew my nose.

"I'm forced to believe you," he said, "hard as it is. You seem genuinely sorry to leave."

I was too choked for speech, but I tried to laugh.

"Why?" he said.

How could I answer?

"We're an unpleasant lot," he said. "You can't have really liked any of us. Except, of course, Amos and Joan."

"You weren't that unpleasant, once we knew each other."

"There were so many forces at work, forces that started in childhood, forces you couldn't begin to understand."

"You mean, the hate you were talking about last night?" He didn't answer. I said slowly, "You mean, the hate you felt for Frances?"

"I don't hate Frances," he said. "When I'm not actively disliking her, I feel sorry for her. She's a pathetic woman. She's never felt secure about herself, she's never believed anyone could love her, and so she's always schemed to put others down so she could have their share of love for herself." His voice was bitter. "It wasn't enough that she share my father's love and respect with us; she had to have it all."

"Did you mind that very much?"

"I did, at one time, when I was younger. Amos minded even more. My father should have listened to Amos when it came to business matters; Amos knows more about the business than any of us. I never cared much for the financial end. My father would say disparagingly that I was the fisherman of the family, but those were Frances' words that my father repeated. And it was Frances that my father listened to when it came to taking that stock out of the business. Amos thinks she did it to spite him, to show him who was most powerful." His smile was one-sided. "Still sorry to leave us?"

I looked out at the snow-dappled fields, the yellow barns, the glimpses of sparkling coves. "Yes."

"You'll forget us soon enough once you have your baby."

My voice sounded unexpectedly small. "I won't have my baby for long."

His head jerked around in surprise. "What do you mean?"

I had assumed he knew. I had never discussed the adoption with anyone but Joan and Amos, but I was sure the others would have found out somehow. "I can't keep the baby," I said. "I can't take care of it and support myself. I have no choice."

My news had dried up the conversation between us. He was still frowning when we reached the airport, and he took my bags and checked them through for me. He walked me to the gate, and now and then I would find his eyes studying me.

He said, "I didn't know, about your baby. I'm sorry."

"I'm used to the idea by now." But my voice shattered.

His frown deepened, his mouth clamped so tight at the corners that two furrows appeared there.

"Anyway, I hope it goes well."

"Thanks."

The last passenger went through the gate.

"I'd better go," I said.

We shook hands. "Have a good trip," he said.

"Thanks," I said again, and went through the gate.

"Daisy!"

My heart leaped into my throat. I turned and went back.

"You'll be careful."

"Of course."

"Will they meet you in New York?"

I almost forgot. "Ernest, would you wire them for me? At the Lanning?"

"I will." He ducked his head abruptly and planted a kiss on my cheek, his face flaming above the brown beard. "Let me know how it goes and where you'll be."

"I will."

My steps felt curiously light as I boarded the plane. When I looked back from the top of the gangplank, he was still there. He wanted to know where I would be. Our taking off was not as painful as it might have been.

VI

☀
☀
☀

1

AT ANOTHER GATE, at another terminal, another
Freer waited for me. Amos; he too kissed my cheek, but
this time all his kiss did was to remind me of Ernest's.

"Are you all right, Daisy? You didn't mind the trip too
much?"

"I'm fine. Just a little tired."

But his appearance shocked me. His face was marked by
strain, that little tic jumping about his mouth. I was almost
afraid to ask: "How's Joan?"

He shook his head at me as if to say, can't you guess?
"Incidentally," he said, "we moved from the Lanning this
morning. I couldn't get a room for you near ours, there's a
convention taking over the place, so we're at the Ballister."

The Ballister turned out to be a small residential hotel.
"It's even closer to the clinic where Joan's going for the
baby," he said. "We have a two-bedroom suite, so I can
keep an eye out for both of you."

We did not have to stop to register but rode up in the

self-service elevator directly to their rooms. As soon as she heard the door opening Joan called out: "Daisy?"

"Coming!"

I hurried to the bedroom. Joan had rouged her cheeks and brushed her hair and tried to cover the dark hollows under her eyes with powder, but she looked sallow and wizened. I tried to hide my dismay.

"What a nice room!"

It was. Furnished in mahogany and chintz, it scarcely looked like a hotel room.

"You're not disappointed that we're not at the Lanning? The Lanning is gayer."

I tried to joke. "Neither of us is going to be in any mood for dancing for the next few days."

She said anxiously, "Daisy, the trip wasn't too much for you? I worried, but Amos checked with Dr. Raab."

"The trip was a breeze." I thought of Ernest and his kiss, and I suppose I must have smiled, because she said, "We're always making unfair demands on you, and you're always so cheerful about them."

"Joan, I'm *glad* to be with you. I'm glad you want me. Tell me, when does the doctor think it will be?"

She said tightly, "Any time now."

"That's wonderful! I wonder which baby will come first."

She shocked me by bursting into hysterical weeping.

Amos was at her side at once. He poured water from a carafe; he produced a capsule. She took it willingly, even eagerly. It must have been powerful, because it began to take effect almost at once. She managed to tell me that Amos had made arrangements for me at a private hospital nearby, but by the time I got around to telling her of Julia and of her reappearance her eyes were dull, and soon she was asleep.

Amos and I tiptoed out and sat down opposite each other in the living room. He gave a despairing shrug.

"She's been this way for the last few days. Crying fits, and then the sedative, and then she sleeps. That's why I felt it so urgent that you come. You're good for her, Daisy. She loves and trusts you. If I didn't know how much she wanted you here, I wouldn't have put you to this inconvenience."

"Oh, Amos, don't even talk about inconvenience. I just wish there was something I could do for her. For both of you."

"You don't know what it means to me just having you here." His smile was forced.

"When did the doctor see her last?"

"He was at the Lanning this morning. I wanted to be sure she could be moved. He said there was nothing more he could do for her, except the sedatives. It's just waiting, now."

"Let's hope it will be soon."

"You must be hungry," he said, rousing himself. "I wish I could take you out at least to a good restaurant, but I don't dare leave her. I've been having my meals sent up. Do you mind very much?"

"Of course not, Amos."

I wasn't as hungry as I should have been. Maybe I was just tired, or maybe their terrible anxiety had quenched what appetite I might have had. I freshened up in the bathroom, examining my face in the mirror. I too showed the effects of the last few hours. What did Ernest think of me?

He had flushed when he kissed me, like a boy. I felt my own face grow warm at the memory. He must like me a little. When I told him last night that I was leaving, he seemed even more disconcerted by the news than by Julia's coming. I felt it intuitively now; I wished I had been as sure before when I was with him, I might have said more. I wondered: Did he guess I was so reluctant to leave because of him?

Dinner had been wheeled in, under silver covers. Amos and I picked at it and drank some wine.

"Amos, what happened since you left? Joan wasn't this bad at Freer's Cove."

"It's just been a long pull, and we're both at the zero of our endurance."

"But it's all so close to the end now. She should be feeling happier that it will soon be over."

"Daisy, give her credit for not being entirely stupid. She knows. She could tell from her last visit to Harcourt that he doesn't give the baby much of a chance."

That was it, of course. Suddenly I felt unendurably tired. I should stay with him, talk with him, try to distract him, but it was too much, and I no longer could muster the energy.

"Amos, I think I'll have to go to bed. The trip took more out of me than I thought."

He was alarmed. "Are you all right? Should you see a doctor? I can call the hotel to send someone up."

I remember the fleeting thought: Why a hotel doctor, why not send for Harcourt, Joan's doctor, but my head was too weary to pursue it. He might have thought a hotel doctor would come more quickly.

"I'm just tired. I'll be all right once I get to bed."

He carried my valise into the bedroom opposite theirs and opened it for me on the luggage rack.

"Is there anything I can get you? I have a flask in my bag. You're sure you're all right?"

"Positive. Amos, why don't you go down for a walk? You look as if you could use some fresh air, and I'll be here in case Joan wakes up and wants something."

"I wouldn't mind getting out for a little while," he admitted.

I took a shower, I looked in on Joan, but she was still sleeping heavily, and I got into bed gratefully, leaving the doors open to both our rooms so that I should hear her if she called, and I fell instantly asleep.

The first pain woke me, unfamiliar, but unmistakable. I didn't move. I waited for the next one, looking at my watch as Dr. Raab had told me to. I didn't want to disturb Amos too soon. It was almost dawn when I felt I could not wait any longer. I put on my robe and went into their bedroom to wake Amos.

He jumped up at once. "What is it, Daisy?"

"It's started. I better get to a hospital right away."

"Don't be frightened," he said. "I've already made arrangements in case this should happen. Can you get dressed by yourself? Do you need any help?"

"I can manage fine."

We had been whispering, but our whispers penetrated Joan's sleep. "Daisy?" she said, opening her eyes.

Amos said, "I have to take Daisy to the hospital, darling. Her baby's on its way. Can you be alone?"

"Of course," said her drug-blurred voice. "Take good care of Daisy. And all the luck in the world."

"I'll share it with you," I said, bending to kiss her.

I dressed, stopping now and then when the pains came, holding on tight until they passed. Amos had already called a taxi; it was waiting for us when we got out of the elevator. We sped through silent graying streets, lit only by the fading streetlights and the occasional splash of color from a neon sign, and directly up through the emergency entrance.

"Is this the hospital where Joan will be going?"

"No, she's going to Harbin's private clinic. He only has room for his own patients."

Harbin? Hadn't he said the doctor's name was Harcourt? But I could have been mistaken, and he, too, under the stress of the moment.

An orderly waited with a wheelchair, and I was put in at once, remaining downstairs in the admissions room only until Amos answered the necessary questions for me and my card was filled out, my wrist braceleted with my name tag. Up in the elevator and into a small private room where I was given a hospital gown to put on while Amos waited somewhere in the corridor. It was happening with extraordinary dispatch; it seemed no time at all when I was being wheeled out of the room again on the surgical cart. They had given me something, and I was drowsy, but Amos appeared beside me just as I was about to be taken up in the elevator.

He kissed me. "Good luck, Daisy. I'll be around when it's over."

The elevator doors shut him away, and I was alone with the nurse and the orderly.

"You're a lucky girl to have such a nice husband," said the nurse.

I only had the strength to shake my head, but she misunderstood.

"Looks like a real doll," she said.

They told me it was a quick and easy delivery, as Dr. Raab had predicted. I remember clearly my child's cry: it seemed to ring in my ears with astonishing vigor through the violet haze I floated in, and I remember saying, "It sounds like a boy." It was. I remember thinking before I went to sleep: If only for a short time at least I will call him James William, after my father, always James, never Jimmy, my father had never been called Jimmy. I remember they showed me his red contorted face, and they said to me, "Isn't he beautiful?" but I did not dare tell them that he was expressing his anger at me for having brought him into these circumstances. I remember Amos' face looking almost happy. "You did it, Daisy. He's a fine one," said his voice, his hand closing over mine.

I awoke to my small sunny room and the phone ringing. There was no one there to tell me I must not answer it, so I reached out for it. It was Joan.

"Amos says you were fine, Daisy. And the baby is perfect."

"It wasn't half as bad as I thought. You're next!"

She said in a small voice, "I wish it were over, all of it."

"It can't be long now."

"Amos is taking me to the clinic tonight. Dr. Harcourt thinks it will be simpler that way. I'm not to receive or make any telephone calls, Daisy, but Amos will keep you in touch."

"I have a feeling everything will work out better than you imagined."

I was still feeling elated. James was neither as red nor as angry as I remembered. When he was brought to me, I gave him his bottle, and he took it reasonably, without undue fuss. He seemed contented and actually pale rather than red-faced. Was he beautiful? I did not think so, but he was a tiny rounded miniature of a baby, with exquisitely curled fingers and toes and a bald round head. I wished his eyes would not be always screwed up.

Amos looked in twice a day. At least once a day he brought me a gift, a lacy bed jacket, lacy handkerchiefs, extravagant bottles of cologne, a procession of fresh bouquets.

"It's too much, Amos!"

"Every new mother should have hordes of visitors bringing flowers and gifts. You have only me, and it's my fault, so please let me try and make it up to you."

Once he brought me an ice-cream soda.

"I'll get fat."

"You've never looked lovelier," he said.

He stopped to see James before he saw me, invariably. "I think James is beginning to know me," he said.

"Impossible!" I laughed. I said more soberly, "*Is* it possible?"

The elation was passing, and one morning I woke up despondent. It was time to think of calling the adoption agency; in matter of fact, it was late. I brought up the question to Amos.

"Wait a day or so. When you're stronger."

"I'm almost ready to leave!"

"Wait," he said. "Wait another day."

The next day he called me and said he would not be in

that day. Joan had started labor. He stammered a little with tension. I was tense myself. At one point I decided I would call him at the clinic. I could talk to him without disturbing Joan. But when I looked up the clinic in the phone book I could not find it. I looked it up under both Harbin and Harcourt and in as many variations of the spelling as I could imagine. I asked the nurse who came in to take my temperature: "Would you know any clinic nearby called Dr. Harbin's? Or Dr. Harcourt's?"

She shook her head. "There are so many in the city. I wouldn't know them all."

Maybe they had an unlisted number. I gathered from both Amos and Joan that Harbin-Harcourt took only a special few cases, and perhaps there was a reason to keep these patients away from reach.

But there was no need to reach him. He turned up after visiting hours for a moment.

"You're going to be discharged tomorrow, Daisy. I'll be here to get you at eleven."

"Wonderful. But tell me, how is Joan?"

He shook his head.

"What does that mean?" I cried.

"We still don't know."

It was already twenty-four hours since she went into labor. My heart sank, but I didn't press him for details. He looked too worn to talk.

They told me at eleven that Amos was waiting for me downstairs. They insisted on putting me back in a wheelchair even though I had been striding along the corridors each day; hospital rules, they said. They dressed James in his elegant satin-trimmed coverall, zipped him up to his chin, put him in my arms, and wheeled me down to where Amos waited.

He held my arm; I held the baby; I walked gingerly. Would I ever be at ease with him; would I ever be able to handle him as if he would not break? Amos seemed as nervous as I was. When he held the baby so that I could get into the car, I thought I saw his hands shake.

I was too busy watching James to observe where we were going, but when I did lift my head, it was to notice that we were in another part of the city, not where the Ballister was.

Surprised, I said, "Where are we going?"

"Don't ask questions. It's a surprise."

I still hadn't asked him about Joan, and he had not volunteered any information. I was afraid to ask now, afraid of what he would tell me. I made myself.

"Amos. How is Joan?"

"She's all right," he said quietly. "You'll see her later."

"The baby?"

He didn't answer at first. The tic jumped in his taut face. "It didn't live."

"When?" I whispered. "When did it happen?"

"Days ago. When she first went into the clinic. I didn't want you upset. It was Joan's idea. She even made up the story about being in labor, because she knew you would wonder what was happening to her and be anxious about her."

I suppose all the time we had really been expecting it. It was not the shock it might have been; it was only terribly sad.

"How is Joan taking it?"

He said evenly, "How do you think?" But he was drawing up to a curb. "Here we are. We'll talk about it later."

It was a pleasant street, with trees on the sidewalk. The apartment house was no longer new, but well kept; there was a canopy at the door, but no doorman. Amos helped me out as carefully as he had put me in, one hand to steady the baby, and he led me into a self-service elevator and up to I don't know which floor and out into a long hall lined with doors and smelling of last night's dinners. He opened a door with his own key.

The room was long, with triple windows at the far end letting in a broad swath of sunlight. The furniture was plain and neat, but on a table was an extravagant bouquet of roses. And in a corner stood a small satin-trimmed basket on wheels. I rushed over to it. On the blue quilted mattress was a blue blanket and a small blue pillow.

"For James. From Joan and me," he said. "Put James down, and then I'll explain."

I unzipped James' coverall and drew him out onto his new bed. He uttered a few sounds of displeasure, yawned, but didn't waken. I sat down. My legs were not as steady as I thought. "Tell me what it means," I said.

He seemed not to know how to begin, moving around uneasily and pointing out this or that. "The kitchenette's in here. I put away whatever you'll need for a few days at least. Joan made up a list. And the hospital gave me a list for the baby, formula, bottles, sterilizer. They'll deliver diapers tomorrow. There's linen service with the apartment. The sofa opens into a bed."

My heart was beating very fast. "Please explain."

He said, "It's yours, Daisy."

I must have looked like a fool. "I don't understand."

He sat down opposite. The sunlight struck him full and showed the pallor of his skin, the tic jumping clearly in his cheek. "Daisy, you asked after Joan. I said she was all right. She's far from all right."

"What is it?"

"Harbin says she can't have any more children."

"Oh, Amos."

"He recommends psychiatric treatment for Joan. He thinks it would help if we adopted a child."

"But that's a wonderful idea!" I cried. "It's what both of you need!"

"It would be cruel to bring an adopted child into that house."

"But why!"

"Because of the way Frances set up the trust."

"Because he won't share in the money?"

"It isn't the money," he said. "Don't you understand? An adopted child has to overcome the feeling that he is different from other children. This damned trust only emphasizes the difference. How will he feel knowing that my father has set aside money for Frances' children, for Maggie and Moira, but not for him? It would be too cruel."

"What does Joan think?"

"Joan doesn't think," he said. "She's constantly under sedation."

Dear God.

"This can't go on," he said. "I can't be with her all the time, can't watch her all the time. She'll need a nurse. The way my mother did." His voice fell away.

"What can I do to help?" I said quietly.

He looked full at me. I thought he might say, come back with us, stay with us, bring the baby and stay. My mind raced: Is this why he asked me to postpone calling the agency?

He said, "Let us have James."

His words knocked the breath out of me.

"I wouldn't ask if I didn't know you're going to give him away anyway. I thought you might be glad. You've become part of us. You know how much we want him, how much we'll love him and care for him. It will be just as if he were born to us. If you say nothing, no one need ever know, not even James."

I was too stunned to think. I mumbled, "The hospital. The birth certificate—"

He said, "You were admitted to the hospital as Joan Freer."

I sat back. So that was why the mistake on my identification bracelet. I hadn't even bothered to read it for several days, and then when I had read Joan's name, I had smiled over it, thinking that Amos had been under such stress when he registered me that he had unconsciously given his wife's name. I was going home in another day when I noticed it, and I had simply let it go. I had assumed the nurses called me Mrs. Freer because of Amos' daily visits; no one had asked questions, and it had seemed easier not to explain.

"And the birth certificate?" I said faintly.

"It says James William Freer."

I felt my face grow hot. He had been under no stress that night; he had planned it that way.

"Daisy, I already knew about Joan. I already knew you

were giving James up. It seemed the perfect answer for both of us. I thought you'd be glad."

Now I understood the look on his face, the anguish, the knowledge of how much hung on my consent.

"We love you, Daisy. We thought you loved us, too. You know the kind of life we can gives James. He'll be a rich man. If you surrender him to an agency, he'll be lost to you forever. You'll never know what became of him, how he grew up, if he's well, happy, successful. This way you'll always be in touch. This way you'll be sure that he has the best of everything. He'll be our own son, Daisy."

I couldn't contain myself. I stood up and went over to the bassinet and looked down on James. I must put out of my mind that this had been planned for me. That wasn't important. What was important was James' happiness. What greater gift could I confer on him than to give him to Amos and Joan? Amos was right. Once surrendered, his whereabouts would be sealed from me forever. I knew the agency would be judicious and painstaking in determining a home for James, but I knew too that as long as I lived I would always wonder: Is he happy, are they good to him, will they love him as I would?

Why did I even hesitate? Keeping him was impossible. And would I be doing the best for *him*, offering him a part-time mother, no father, or at best a stepfather?

Again Amos had stepped into the breach, as he had that first day I met him, and offered a clear-cut solution to my problems, a solution far better than any I could have dreamed of.

I said, "I'd like you to have him."

His face underwent a transformation. It was as if with

a few words I had been able to erase the marks of months of tension and anxiety and fear. His eyes actually had tears in them.

"What can I say?" His voice was thick. "What can I say, Daisy?"

He came up to me and put his arms around me and kissed me.

"How can we ever make it up to you, Daisy? We want to do everything. This apartment. It's yours for as long as you need it, until you can support yourself. We will take care of your bills at the university, there'll be money deposited in a checking account in your name for whatever incidental expenses you will have—"

I hardly heard him. Now that the decision was made I felt suddenly exhausted. I wanted nothing more than to be alone.

Amos saw I was tired. He pulled out the folding bed from the sofa for me. "Maybe you've overdone it for today, Daisy. Why don't you get into bed? We'll leave you alone. There's a restaurant down the street, I'll have them send dinner up to you. There's just the baby's bottles— Can you manage them?"

"Of course, Amos."

"Is there anything else I can do?"

He was so excited and happy and stirred and anxious all at once. My voice softened.

"Nothing, Amos. You've thought of everything."

He hesitated. "Daisy, the sooner, the better, right? A quick, clean break?"

I nodded.

"We'll be here in the morning," he said. "We love you, Daisy. See you in the morning."

I made my first batch of bottles. James was making increasingly fretful sounds, and I fed him and put him on my shoulder as I had learned to do until he had brought up his bubble. I changed him, taking an age with the diaper so as not to pinch him, and put him back in his quilted bed with the ribbons that must have cost one of my weeks' pay and was a kind of symbol of the life that lay ahead for him.

Day faded and became dusk; my hot dinner arrived, and I ate a little and thriftily put the rest in the refrigerator for tomorrow. It was night, and I did not turn on the lamps, but the electric sign on top of the building opposite threw a cheerful red glow through the net curtains into my apartment. Now and then James gave a tiny snort in his sleep like a puppy, and I would jump up and see if he was dry, or offer him some water, or feed him when it was time. He was very obliging, making few demands; it was almost as if he recognized the imperative that we have as little to do with each other as possible, that the less we touched, the easier it would be for us to part. The less I remembered of his small weight pressed against my arm, of his curled legs, of the touch of silk down on the soft part on top of his head, the better for us both. I did not want him to have conflicting memories of another mother when Joan held him, fed him, changed him. . . .

It will be as if I had never borne him, as if he had never existed. I can resume my life without a single apprehension, a single doubt. We will both be beautifully taken care of.

I lay in bed and thought. And thought. If it had all worked out so beautifully for me, it had all worked out equally beautifully for Joan and Amos. It was almost as if it had been planned.

Planned. He had entered me in the hospital as his wife; it was simpler that way. The birth certificate in the name of Freer. Long ago, when he had first helped me take my leave from Jed, from New York, he had said, *"It's the small details that people forget."* Amos was a precise man; he would think of small details. And large details.

They had always believed their child would not be born or would not live. They had found a companion for Joan, providentially one about to have a child at about the same time, one who did not have a husband to claim that child, one who had said over and over and over again that she did not intend to keep her baby, that it would be turned over for adoption. Hadn't he actually seen her for the first time in that adoption agency then and there ready to make the arrangements? Whatever happened to Joan, he had arranged that a baby be ready for adoption, arranged it in such a way that no one could possibly know it was not their own. They knew that my love and gratitude for them would seal their secret.

Their baby—my baby—would share in the trust. Amos would have a handsome income from it for twenty-one years.

Thoughts proliferated, one growing out of the other, pounding in my head so that I could not sleep. Wasn't it a coincidence that our babies were to be born the same week, within days of each other? How could he have planned for that? Unless— Who was Dr. Harcourt? Or Dr. Harbin? Was there a clinic? Was Joan a patient there? Unless— *Had she ever been pregnant at all?*

I threw off the blanket, so disturbed I could not lie still. All, all an elaborate plot to take James? No, I would not allow myself to think that. I remembered their months of anxiety, of Joan's sick fear. *But why was she afraid? Of what?*

I stopped and stared at my son, lit rosily by the lights from the illuminated sign across the way.

Suppose my suspicions were true, suppose I had rightly reconstructed their plan, what difference should it make, to James or me? No matter how deviously they had schemed to obtain him, no matter what benefit they would derive from having him, I knew they wanted him as their own son, and they would love him as much as I could. Nothing else should matter to me.

2

Amos telephoned at nine. "How are you? And James?"

"Fine."

"Can you have him ready in about an hour?"

"Yes."

"I'll be there in an hour."

I had James sponged and dressed, fed and dry, in plenty of time. I no longer needed the small overnight bag for the hospital. I repacked it with only James' things. He did not really need the clothes I had bought him; there would be an extravagant layette waiting for him at Freer's Cove, and more of the best to come. But what use were his few things to me, and it would be comforting to think of him wearing some of the clothes I had been able to provide for him. I folded the diapers on top neatly, and some of the changes he might need during the trip, smoothing them carefully. It was the last service I would provide for my son. I refolded them; I touched them again, until I made myself stop and closed the bag. It was as if I wanted to do something more for him, but there was nothing.

Amos rang the bell and came in. He did not even take off his coat, but I made him wait.

"Amos, suppose they ask about me. Frances will. Even . . . even Ernest might."

"Are they likely to?" He looked surprised. "You'll have disappeared from their lives completely, as you will from ours. On the surface from ours, anyway. But no one will know about the apartment or the checking account."

"I don't want the apartment. Or the checking account," I said in a small voice. "Maybe just for a month, until I find a job. But I can take care of myself." This was another of the thoughts that had revolved in my brain last night: I had hardly slept at all. "I'm not . . . selling James."

"Oh, Daisy, why should you feel that way? Joan and I can't do enough for you. We *want* to do it for you. You're saving Joan's sanity for us both. We're not putting a price on that, any more than on James. We want you to have it, whatever we can do to make you happy."

Make me happy. But I was too distracted to argue then. "They'll ask after my baby, your father, Frances. Ernest. What will you tell them?"

"That he died," he said quietly.

He saw my face.

"Daisy, this will be the best way. Don't you think I've thought about it often?"

How often? How long is it that you've been thinking about it?

"You don't want James ever to find out that he isn't our son, do you? You wouldn't want him hurt that way."

Or you. You wouldn't want to lose that income from the trust. No, I mustn't think of that. That has nothing to do with James or me.

I zipped James into his coverall.

"I wouldn't let Joan come up. In case there were these questions. But you bring the baby down to her, Daisy. I think it would be better. You'll want to say good-bye to her anyway, and this way you'll be *giving* James to her, see, giving him yourself. She won't think that she's *taking* him from you."

James had squirmed around, so the hood was half over his face. I unzipped him and rearranged it. This is it, James. Remember, I'm doing us both a favor, but especially you. This may be the best thing a mother ever did for her child. Who wouldn't choose for her baby the kind of life that you're going to have? You're among the chosen few, James, the top percentile of the population when it comes to worldly goods. You're going to be one of the elite. And you won't even be left with a memory of me. Her hands will feel just like mine, maybe not as clumsy. Her smell will be like mine; Amos bought me the same cologne and bath powder she uses. Maybe he even thought of that in his plans; maybe he was even worried about your memories, too.

He yawned, screwing up his eyes and mouth.

How to explain myself? Crazy Daisy. Jed had said it long ago. I never seem to be able to do what is best, even when I know it, which isn't often. Married on impulse, separated on

impulse, pregnant by accident, Freer's Cove an accident—
I had brought this baby into the world against all tenets of
logic and common sense, and now, *now*, against all tenets of
logic and common sense, I could not give him up.

I did not dare turn around. I did not dare show him my
face. I would have hidden from him if I could, taken James,
and locked myself up somewhere where he wouldn't see on
my face that I couldn't give James to him.

I had promised. And these were my friends. I made myself
face him.

"Amos, I can't do it."

He didn't understand. "What?"

"Please understand. I just can't."

The room was utterly still.

He said slowly, "Daisy, you're not thinking straight."

"I know. I'm not thinking at all. It's all feeling now."

The look on his face was so despairing that it frightened
me. "How will I tell her?" he said.

"Let me tell her. She'll understand when I tell her. She
knows what it would be for me; she's been through it herself;
she can put herself in my place—" I must sound as an-
guished as he did.

"No. Wait," he said. I had started to put on my coat. "Let
me think. I must think." He sat down.

I tried to guess what was happening behind his still, set
mask of face. His eyes had always had a secret inscrutable
life behind that gray glance; now they were utterly blank.
Only the little tic jumped in his cheek.

Remorse overpowered me. I had done this to them, my
friends, who had given me so much. Why had they given
me so much, so that I would give them my baby? No, I had

been prepared to give the baby up to strangers, to an impersonal agency; it was not their stratagem that I give up my baby, it was my own idea. Giving them the baby was the best—

"Please let me talk to Joan."

"You don't understand," he said in a dead voice. "This will destroy her."

I started to say something else, but he cut me short. He said sharply, "*Let me think!*"

He was precise, he was disciplined, he was tenacious; he would have a plan, he would devise something. Sick with remorse, shaking with the enormity of my decision, I waited.

"Will you do one last favor for me?"

I met his eyes. I said with dry mouth, "Whatever I can."

"Then do this. Don't tell her yet."

"But you're leaving—"

"Come with us. Tell Joan you want to be with James one more day, tell her how hard it is for you to give him up. It won't be so sudden. You mean a great deal to Joan; she won't want to hurt you. She'll see how strongly you feel, wanting just one more day. She'll be sorry for you. We'll plan to spend the night somewhere on the way. In the morning you'll tell her. But by that time maybe she'll have guessed it herself. You'll see. She'll tell you to keep James. I know her."

It was reasonable. She couldn't stand another shock. But if she saw how desperately I had to keep James, she would come around herself. Amos planned well. His mind could anticipate; it concerned itself with small details.

"All right, I'll come with you," I said. "But in the morning—"

"In the morning we'll drive you to the railroad station and you'll take the first train back to New York. And this apartment. The rent is paid for the month anyway."

There was no point in taking my clothes. I opened the overnight bag and slipped some toilet articles on top of James's things. I left the big valise still strapped; I hadn't yet unpacked it.

"You have bottles for him?"

I pointed to the thermal bag.

"I'll carry the bassinet," Amos said. "He can use it on the trip."

I followed with James.

Joan was waiting in the car; she began to smile almost at once when she saw James. I had never seen that kind of smile on her face during the whole time I had known her.

"I can't believe it, Daisy. I can't believe he's ours."

I couldn't speak. Amos explained. I marveled at his glibness, knowing the turmoil he must be feeling.

"Daisy finds it hard to say good-bye to James. I told her to come along with us, and stay with him a little while longer. She'll take the train home herself."

Not myself. With James. But of course he wanted that decision to come from Joan.

She sat in the back with me, the bassinet propped up on the floor between us. Now and then she would ask if she could hold James, or diaper him, or give him his bottle.

"I want to get used to him. And get him used to me."

I let her, but it hurt me to see her pleasure, knowing it couldn't last. Amos' plan could fail; it might be harder rather than easier for her to relinquish him.

I had time to think about the practical aspects of my

position. The money I had saved would go for food and rent. If I found a job, who would take care of James? If I budgeted carefully to make the money last even a year, how could I go back to school, how could I afford to pay someone to care for him? And what about the doctor? Babies need to be seen by a doctor regularly. And there were injections. And vitamins. What would I do for money?

A thought occurred to me: Did Amos have this in mind? Was this part of the plan, that *I* might reconsider, rather than Joan? Was he counting on my practicality coming to the fore, once I had time to think?

We didn't take the turnpike, which was fast, and which would have brought us to Freer's Cove by night. If she arrived with the baby that night, she would have to tell them that it was hers; then how could she give him back to me? So we took the small roads, through lovely farm country just wakening to spring, through mountains still covered with snow, through the damp soft look of New England villages just digging out from the winter. We reached the New Hampshire coast by dark.

To Amos' dismay he discovered that most of the motels in this summer-oriented region were closed for the season. We all were tired by now, and restless, and James seemed to sense our tension and began a thin wailing cry. At last we came to a stretch of coast road where, in addition to the gray boarded-up beach houses scattered along it, was the welcome red neon sign glowing up ahead: MOTEL.

We drove up. The scattered cottages were dark, and there were no cars drawn up in front of them. Only the office had

the motel sign lighted up on top of it, and even as Amos got
out of the car, the light was turned off.

"Damn," he said. "I bet they're closed."

The office door opened and slammed shut; a man emerged;
Amos sprinted, and caught him before he could get into
his car. They both returned to the office together, and a light
was turned on again.

"I don't like it here," said Joan. "I don't like all those dark
trees."

"Oh, Joan. After Freer's Cove."

"It looks dingy. Grimy."

"It's just for the night." But I would not have chosen to
stay there myself.

Amos returned, waving two keys triumphantly. "Just
caught him in time," he said. "He's only the caretaker, keeps
an eye out in case there might be a stray tourist. Only keeps
open till nine. The owners are in Florida."

He drove slowly, searching for the numbers over the
cabin doors. There were no lights, and the trees blocked our
vision. We found the two cabins, fairly close together, and a
stone walk connecting them; Amos left the car in the road
below.

"Let's get Daisy and James settled in hers first," he said,
going ahead with the key. Joan and I carried the bassinet
with James in it between us.

The cabin was not as bad as we imagined. There were
webs in the corners and a smell of damp wood, damp bed-
ding, but the electric heater warmed the room fast and dis-
sipated the odor. In the tiny living room was a wicker set,
and in back a bedroom and a bathroom with a tin shower. I

peered through the blind, but I could see nothing outside but a dense stand of trees and a stubble of underbrush.

"It'll do nicely for tonight, Joan."

She was huddled near the heater. Amos had brought the overnight bag in and then left for the other cabin with their valise. He returned in a few minutes.

"I'm going to take a run down the road with the car. The caretaker said there was a truck stop open about five miles down where we can get something to eat. James is provided for, right, Daisy?"

He was trying very hard to sound casual and brisk, but it didn't quite come off, and I felt sorry for him.

"You stay here with Daisy, Joan. It's warm already, and I'll bring the food back here."

After he left, I took care of James, making him comfortable, heating his bottle by letting it stand in hot running water, the best I could do.

Joan was watching me. It was almost as if she had waited for Amos to go, so she could speak more freely.

"Do you mind very much giving up James?"

I was disconcerted. I looked at her, but her face was composed. She looked oddly calm, as if a storm had passed over and she were left worn but quiet. It was what Amos had said might happen. If she knew what James meant to me, she would come around herself.

"Yes," I said. "Very much."

"Of course you do," she said. "It was stupid of me to ask." She watched me slip a clean shirt over James' head. "If only we could help you to keep him," she said.

I leaned back. Was she making only conventional words of sympathy, or did she mean what she was saying?

I hesitated. I knew she would have to be told sooner or later, Amos had promised he would tell her today, but I would have wished Amos were here when she found out, in case she broke down, became hysterical. . . . And yet as I looked at her she seemed more tranquil than I had ever seen her. That gave me the courage to speak.

I said, "I know how mad it seems, even to me, to think of keeping him. But—oh, Joan, I can't bear to give him up!"

I could hear no sound in the cottage.

Finally she said, quietly, "Does Amos know how you feel?"

"Yes."

She got up and walked to the window and stood there, her back to me, looking down the road from where Amos would come.

My mind whirled: Will she reason with me as Amos did, plead as he did, will she cry, will she be angry? She faced me.

"Let me help you keep him, Daisy."

I was speechless. I stammered, "Amos—" I stopped.

"Amos doesn't have to know," she said. "I have money of my own. You can pay it back once you're able to work."

I could only stare at her, trying to comprehend what she was saying. I said, "But don't you *want* him?"

"More than anything in the world," she said. "More than you can possibly guess. Or can you? You must know already how important this baby is for Amos. But I only agreed to take him because Amos said from the first you were going to give him up to an agency."

"But Amos said—" I caught myself short again. Amos had said her very sanity depended on her having my baby.

"How could I take him from you if you want him?" she said.

I found my voice. "What will you tell Amos?"

She met my eyes for a long moment. "I don't know that yet."

It was then that I realized that she must know everything, whatever had happened this last year, she knew more than any of us. I felt cold, suddenly, and I didn't dare question her any further. I think I was afraid to hear what she knew.

But she went on without my asking her, as if we both must face the ultimate truth now. Her voice was still quiet, with a kind of despairing calm.

"Amos wants your child," she said. "He planned it that way from the beginning, step by step. Whatever month your baby would come, mine would come at the same time."

It was true.

"I miscarried again, in the fourth month. We both knew then I could never have another child. We never told anyone. Amos thought of this plan. His mind is methodical. He thought it out, from beginning to end. It was the only way we could carry it off, that it was our own baby, the only way we could be sure no one would suspect."

My mind still couldn't comprehend the enormity of the ruse. "All those months in bed—"

"I could fool everyone better that way," she said in that dead voice. "It seemed natural enough, I was always frail, Frances knew that."

I tried to think. "But *why*, Joan? Just for the trust fund? You and Amos have enough without that!"

"Oh, Daisy. Can you actually believe it might be for the money? If it had been only the money I might have reasoned with him. It goes so much deeper. It was all *his father*. It was *Frances.*"

"Why? *Why?*"

"How can I try to explain why he felt as he did? I don't understand it myself. Only it drove him, it . . . eroded his very soul, Daisy. He wanted that baby for his father, like an offering. His father wanted a son from Amos, and Amos couldn't bear to fail him!"

I said slowly, "But Frances?"

"Don't you see, she was the one who drove him the hardest? She always tried to take their father's love for herself. It didn't matter in the beginning, when his father appreciated Amos' part in the business, but later, when the business ceased to matter to Father, it was only the children that were important. They were Frances' weapon against Amos. She was the only one to give Father grandchildren. The only one Father loved."

She looked into my stricken face, and suddenly her calm deserted her. "I had to do it for Amos! He begged so! It was my fault we had no children. I drove him to this!"

I whispered, "Frances' children—"

"He would have loved them; he did, I think, in his way. He only could . . . hurt them because of her."

I could scarcely hear her last words, yet the enormity rang and rang in my ears.

We stared at each other as Amos' car came to a stop in the drive below. She moved away from the window, as if she didn't want him to know she was watching for him; she composed her face.

Amos came in with a brown paper bag which he put down on the table. "That's our dinner, I'm afraid. All I could find open was a greasy spoon joint, but they made me some sandwiches, and they had cold beer on ice. It's the best I could do."

He sensed something in our silence. His forced heartiness fell away. He walked heavily into the bathroom to get some glasses.

It was a silent meal. He was supposed to help Joan to change her mind about James, but he said nothing, and it was almost as if he knew we knew.

"We're all tired," he said, when I cleared the bag and the cans away from the table and into the wastepaper basket. "Let's let Daisy get to sleep, and we'll make an early start in the morning. We'll have to get her to a railroad station so she can get back to New York."

Not even Daisy and her baby? Just Daisy? Was it a slip, or did he sense I knew, and there was no more pretending, no more scheming, no more plans?

Only a last plan.

He would take James. *What did he intend to do with me?*

We said our good-nights. I closed and locked the door behind them. My throat was dry with fear. I watched them through the slats of the blind making their way along the stone path to their cottage. Is there going to be another accident, Amos?

I knew only one thing, I must take James and run. Blind animal instinct told me that. Get out. Run. Hide.

But he would be watching. He would wait until he thought I was asleep. If I left the cabin now, he would come for me. But there was Joan. I tried desperately to be logical, as he was, I tried to put myself into his brain. But reason has never been my dominant trait, and besides, I was terrified.

He would not want Joan to know. He would have to do whatever he did when she was asleep. I had some time. I must think. Make for the highway? But it wasn't a highway; it was a narrow piece of seaside road used only in the summer. I had not heard a single car pass in the entire time I had stood by the window. Amos must have chosen this way deliberately; he might even have known of the cabins. There was only one place to hide. In the woods. If I had sufficient time to get far enough away.

Feverishly I began to dress James in whatever warm clothes I had brought. He whimpered, but I patted him to sleep again. I had nothing but Julia's red coat, but fortunately it went half again around me now that I was slim again.

I turned out my light and lay down across the bed until I should see their light go out.

3

There was a thin tap on my door. I sat up. Through the drawn blinds I could see Amos' cabin in darkness. Again the sound, a fingernail tapping on wood. I got to my feet silently and crept to the window and peered out through an opening in the curtains.

Joan.

For an instant I hesitated, afraid to open the door even to her. No, I had to trust her.

"Daisy!" she was whispering urgently. "Hurry!"

I opened the door a crack and drew her inside.

"I haven't a moment. He allowed himself to fall asleep for a little while, still in his clothes. Take James and run!"

She needed no more explanation.

"Come with us, Joan."

"He won't hurt me." Now I heard her crying, shivering in her thin robe. "He's sick. He needs me. He loves me, Daisy; he won't hurt me."

"What is he going to do to me?"

"I don't know. He told me you were planning to take the sleeper from Canada; it goes through not far from here early in the morning; he said you asked him to put you on it while I was still asleep. He said you wanted it that way, that you were thinking of me, that you didn't want me to be upset over your leaving James with me. I knew you wouldn't leave James with me; I knew he was lying." She pulled at my arm. "Hurry. He might wake up and miss me!"

Paralyzed with fear, I repeated, "What is he going to do with me?"

"He must have a plan. He always has a plan. Like with the children!"

I had to believe it. "Amos—The children. . . . Every time?"

"Not Ronnie," she whispered. "Ronnie was an accident. Amos wouldn't have hurt Ernest's child. But it must have given him the idea. I would see him sit by himself, thinking, his face . . . it was terrible, Daisy! I was so afraid! I told myself he couldn't. Not Amos. But he's very sick, Daisy. I know that now. He didn't go to sleep after Thanksgiving dinner. He left me alone. I watched from the window. He went to the barn. And that night Maggie—He didn't sleep then either. He pretended. He was out in the fog. Oh, please go quickly, Daisy!"

I picked up James dazedly.

"Not the door! The window in the back! He may be watching!"

The window creaked as I tugged at it. I opened it inch by inch, so he would not hear, until there was space for me to slip through. "Hold James." I put one leg over the sill and swung the other after it, and dropped to the ground.

She leaned down and put James into my arms. "Run!"

Behind me I could hear the window closing with the same terrifying care.

And then I heard it, like the crack of a pistol in the quiet night: A door opened and banged shut. At once, running feet. Amos. He was making for my cabin. He had missed Joan. I could hear the pebbles skittering from under his shoes.

No time to run. He would hear me in the underbrush. I looked around wildly. I couldn't reach another cabin. He would see me, and I would be trapped. I was rooted there in terror. And then my frantic glance found it.

A rotting lattice surrounded the crawl space under the cabin. Part of it bulged out, leaving a small opening. I didn't stop to think, I moved instinctively, clawing at the lattice until there was a space wide enough for me to get through. I pushed James in as far as I could reach, and crawled in on my stomach after him, and with shaking fingers pulled the lattice back as tight as it would go, to conceal my entrance. Like an animal trapped in his burrow I retreated back inch by inch, holding James under my arm, back, back, back, away from the faintest light.

My elbow sank into ooze. I had come to a place where the hot-water pipes drained down from the cabin. With my gorge rising in revulsion I inched away to where the ground was still frozen and lay still so I could examine James. He seemed unhurt, almost completely covered except for a small section of his face. Miraculously he seemed asleep, unless my fear had communicated itself to him and he was shocked into stillness.

Overhead I heard their voices, hollow and distorted.

"What are you doing here? Where are they?"

"I came to see if James was all right. But they were gone."

"Where did they go? When did they go?"

"I don't know. They were gone when I came here. The door was open."

Silence.

"Go back to bed, Joan. It's cold. I'll look for them."

"Let them go."

"It isn't like Daisy to act so stupidly. She shouldn't have taken a chance with a week-old baby."

"Please let them go, Amos."

Their muffled voices rang and echoed above me.

"She's not strong yet, and it's too cold for the baby. She couldn't have gone very far."

"*Please, Amos.*"

"You wouldn't want anything to happen to the baby, Joan."

I heard her sobbing. I heard him leave the cabin, racing down the wooden steps, running for the car. My breath exploded inside me with relief. He's going to look for me on the road! But he came back to the cabin, a circle of light dancing in front of him. He had only gone for the flashlight.

It seemed as if he must hear my agonized breathing, the thumping of my heart, across the small intervening distance. I wrapped my stole around James; if he whimpered, I would have to muffle him. But wouldn't Amos hear, in the complete stillness? Suppose he heard . . . He would have to crawl in after me to kill me.

The flashlight played around the ground near the wooden steps, as if he hoped to trace my prints. But there were too many. The light moved toward the lattice, played there, but only halfheartedly, as if he could not even conceive that I would be there. Still, he walked around uncertainly, the dancing light streaking through the lattice, but not far enough to reach me.

He was moving away. I allowed myself to expel a sobbing breath. He was hurrying toward another cabin farther on; I could hear his steps ringing on the stone paths. He moved on, half running now. He was using his key on other doors and opening them; faintly I could hear the sounds of his desperate search. His blind, furious haste terrified me . . . it was mindless, it was . . . mad.

From where I lay I could see him run down the slope toward the car.

"Amos!" Joan cried his name, but he did not stop. Gravel expelled explosively from under the tires as he was off.

I lay frozen. Crawl out now, run into the woods. But Joan would hear. She would not willingly tell him where we were, but he might make her. Stay. He had not found us here before; if he searched again when he came back, he might not find us again.

I heard the car return. I could see Amos move slowly up the slope, up to the cabin. Joan was waiting for him on the steps. I could not see them now, only hear her run to him.

His voice was strangely dull. "It was so dark. How could I ever find her in the dark?"

"It will be all right, Amos."

He said, *"But she has our baby, Joan."*

In the horrible quiet I could hear her crying. "We'll have one of our own, darling. Come inside."

Her crying, his voice, his words, stayed inside my head after their door had closed behind them. I was crying myself, but I didn't notice until I felt my stole wet with tears. I patted James, lest he sense my anguish, but I did not dare stir. Things crawled on my face, I brushed them off, a small animal scampered near me, but I did not move, too paralyzed with grief and fear to notice or care. I kept hearing his voice, *"she has our baby,"* and it was the voice of a madman.

VII

T HE LIGHT GRAYED, and I knew it would soon be morning. I tried to move my stiff body, and James whimpered. He would soon be hungry. I rocked him as well as I could and patted desperately, and miraculously he lapsed back into sleep.

Their cabin door opened; I heard them coming down the path. Then Joan was all right, at least. Car doors shut, and the car moved away. I felt like an animal in a burrow and behaved with the same cunning. They might come back. This might be a trap. I did not move.

It must have been hours later when I heard the car. But it did not sound like the humming motor of Amos' car; it rattled and choked and came to a stop farther down near the office. Still, I did not move.

Footsteps approached my cabin; I hardly breathed. And then I saw **stout** legs in sensible oxfords clomp up the wooden steps. Windows were opened; water ran; someone was cleaning up.

Gingerly, sorely, I crawled to my providential bit of lattice and pushed it out. I could hardly stand up on my cold, cramped feet.

An astonished face peered down at me through the open window, a round red old face, under a bird's nest of gray hair.

"Where did you come from? And with a little baby!"

My voice cracked when I spoke. "This was my cabin. Is there a telephone somewhere?"

She was so bemused by my appearance that she had to rouse herself. "In the office. It's open."

Shifting James in my stiff arms, I made my way down to the office. I did not consciously think of calling Ernest; I heard myself call information and ask for the number of the Fisheries, and when they answered my ring, I heard myself ask for Ernest Freer.

"Hello?"

I had not realized how my legs were trembling until I heard his voice. "Ernest, this is Daisy."

An endless moment, and then he said, "Where are you?"

"I don't know." I was holding on hard to what self-control I had left. "Wait—" A stack of postcards on the desk read THE SEACREST MOTEL, PORTWAY, NEW HAMPSHIRE. I told him.

"What are you doing there?"

"I can't tell you over the phone. Can you come here, quickly?"

His voice changed, flattened, quickened. "What happened? Are you in trouble?"

"Amos—" I stopped.

The pause was longer this time. He said, "They drove up as I was leaving. I tried to speak to them, but Joan drove on without stopping." Another pause. "Can you wait there?"

"But please hurry."

"I'm leaving now."

The cleaning woman came puffing into the office with the bassinet, my purse, my bag. "These yours?" I nodded. Her glance was curious. "Can I get you something? Looks like you could use some hot coffee."

She was stout, and normal, and kind, and *safe*, the way people used to be, before I came to Freer's Cove. I watched her plug in a coffeemaking machine on the wall and return with hot coffee, and I felt an impulse to weep and to kiss her.

"I have to give the baby his bottle."

"Give it to me, dear. I can warm it on the burner."

I took the warmed bottle she brought me and fed James. She watched me unzip him and change him, and put him into his bassinet. He seemed none the worse for his night, unlike me. She said, "You with the people in the other cabin last night?"

I nodded.

"Friends of yours, and went off and left you here with a baby and no car to get home?"

"Someone is coming for me," I said faintly.

She was plainly mystified, but she patted my shoulder, and said, "I'd better finish cleaning up. Why don't you wash and fix you hair before your friend comes?" She looked down at the bassinet before she left. "My, isn't he the beautiful baby!"

I went into the washroom. No wonder the cleaning woman had looked at me that way. My face was scratched and streaked with mud, my hair matted and dried leaves stuck to it; my coat was filthy. I cleaned my face, I combed my hair, I scrubbed at my coat with a paper towel and water, I wiped my boots; I was beginning to feel calmer.

Obligingly, James had fallen asleep. How lucky for us both that newborn babies sleep so much. "You were very nice to be so quiet last night," I whispered to him. It was as if he had known our lives hung on it.

I was at the window watching for him when Ernest's car hesitated at the motel sign and then turned in. I opened the door.

"Ernest!"

He seemed to leap out of the car and come running almost before it came to a full stop. He came at me at top speed, and when he reached me, he seemed to catch himself. Later I thought, he would have taken me in his arms; only he must have realized, what right have I? Have we come so far in such a short absence, after such an early stormy acquaintance? I thought that later; now I started to smile at him, only I was crying. His hands gripped my arms.

"The baby?"

"Fine," said my shaky voice, "see for yourself." Only when his grip on my arms relaxed and he went toward the bassinet did I become aware that my arms hurt with his pressure.

"Amos said he died," Ernest said, looking down at James.

I drew in my breath. "When did he tell you?"

"Some days ago. When I finally found the hotel. I felt like all manner of fool when I let you go that morning on the plane. But if I had told you my suspicions, you wouldn't have believed me, and I couldn't have proved them." He looked at me, and the blood crept back under his tanned skin. "But you're all right?"

"I am now." I took another shaky breath and then told him everything. We sat on the stiff upholstered settle opposite the motel reception desk, with its stack of innocent postcards and its assorted credit card shields and its rack of fruit drops and chewing gum and stomach pills, and my faltering account of last night and what had preceded it seemed even more bizarre in contrast. But I was only filling in the details for him; he had half suspected the general plan. The only time he swore was when I described my lying under the cabin with the baby; even telling him that Joan had lost the baby earlier only made the lines in his forehead deeper.

"He concealed it all so well," he said. "His desperation. And yet it drove him out of his mind. My own brother. I knew something was wrong, but I never guessed how wrong. Even when I tracked him down in New York—"

"How did you manage?"

"By calling every hotel. Fortunately he used his right name in checking in. I suppose he never imagined I would try to reach him. Why should he? How could he imagine that I"—he stumbled a little here, and more blood surged up from under his brown beard—"that I would worry about you."

Why should that make tears start again in my eyes? He looked at me, and I saw his hands tighten on his thighs. I whispered, "How did you know . . . about Amos?"

"I never *knew*. It was only a feeling. That Thanksgiving day before Jeffrey drowned. Amos said he wanted to catch a nap before driving to New York. I was roaming the property, and I saw him. It was almost dark, and he was coming from the barn. We keep the saws there. He kept to the trees, in the dark places, and went into the house through the kitchen, which was dark."

His mouth tightened, and he was silent, remembering. I could see he suffered for Amos, but there was nothing I could do to help him.

He said, "There was that night we found Maggie. I could see his face clearly in the floodlights when he saw me carrying her. His expression only lasted a moment, but I think I knew then. Still, how could I be sure?"

I too was reconstructing that evening. "If Amos had stood outside and whistled for Brownie, Brownie would have come. Amos was with Brownie a lot."

"We kept fishnetting in the barn. He could have ripped some off to wrap Brownie in and stowed him down among the rocks. He could have kept just enough ahead of Maggie to stay out of sight. He might even have been down there waiting, when she fell. That earth and snow were frozen; they couldn't have given way. It had to be dug away and then packed lightly back so it would give."

But how could anyone believe it of Amos? Ernest echoed my thought aloud. "I suppose I didn't want to believe it. We were always . . . we loved each other." His voice fell away.

I swallowed. "He never let Frances say a word against you."

"I can imagine she tried," he said wryly. "And after all, I was the one with the temper, the one who'd gone off the deep end."

"Amos never touched Ronnie. Joan told me."

"I never thought he did," he said, and for an instant his face crumpled. He recovered. "But I think he got the idea from **Ronnie.** The pattern of accident. A child died; it was an accident—But it could have been planned; it could have been deliberate."

Again his eyes rested on me. Suffused with feeling—could they ever have been as coldly cynical as I imagined them?

"I think he planned to kill you," he said thickly. "I think the collapse of his hopes for your baby unhinged him completely. I don't think he was able anymore to plan your death as an accident, and he couldn't stop at anything at this point."

I said, my voice faint with the enormity, "What will happen to him now?"

He turned away. "Jeffrey can't be brought back to life. And Frances will want to shield my father. And the family. Whatever is done with Amos, it will be quiet, without scandal—"

"In a way, I was responsible," I said. "If I hadn't promised—"

"Don't ever think that, Daisy!"

He put his hand over my mouth. I don't know whether it was his touching me or whether he finally had to let me know that he would be there from now on if I wanted him, to shield me, to love me, but I put my face down onto his shirtfront, and his arms went around me, and I knew that I never wanted to be farther away from him than this, and I sensed it was the same with him. Dimly I was aware that the cleaning woman looked in at the door and then went away, but neither of us moved, nothing was as important.

It was James' peremptory cry that finally made us draw apart. He was all right; his face unscrewed and his mouth sucked a few times, but he slipped back into sleep. I pushed my hair away from my face. Reality returned. "I should start back to New York."

"Do you have a place to stay?"

I thought of the apartment that Amos had taken for me, and I shuddered. I would have to take my valise from it, but I would never stay in it any more time than that took.

"I might fly down to Florida and stay with my aunt for a while." Wasn't that Amos' idea? But like all his ideas, so logical.

He got up and stood beside me, looking down at James. "Florida's far away."

I nodded. Don't let me go to Florida, Ernest. Ask me to stay here, near you.

"Don't go to Florida, Daisy. Not now."

I nodded again, knowing it was all on my face, what I felt, just as it was on his.

"I have a friend who lives in Brunswick, near the college," he said. "She rents out rooms to students, and I know she'll find something for you if I ask her. I can drive you there right now. If you want me to."

I found my voice. "Yes, I'd like that."

His hand found mine and closed on it. "I'll come weekends," he said. "And maybe during the week after work. The pike is fast, and Brunswick is pretty close. This way, I can look in on you often to see how you're doing, you and James."

"It sounds wonderful."

"You mean that, Daisy."

"Every word."

"Well," he said quietly, "then that's settled. What are we waiting for?"